# THE LAST VOYAGE OF SIGISMUND SKRIK

# THE LAST VOYAGE OF SIGISMUND SKRIK

**KARSTEN FLOHR**

*Translated by John Brownjohn*

amazon crossing

This is a work of fiction. Names, characters, organizations, places, events, and incidents are either products of the author's imagination or are used fictitiously.



Previously published as *Die letzte Fahrt des legendären Schiffsfrisörs Sigismund Skrik* by the author via the Kindle Direct Publishing Platform in Germany in 2013. Translated from German by John Brownjohn. First published in English by AmazonCrossing in 2015.

Published by AmazonCrossing, Seattle

www.apub.com



ISBN-13: 9781477830871

ISBN-10: 1477830871

Cover design by David Drummond

Library of Congress Control Number: 2015900339

Printed in the United States of America

# 1

# *Wherever there's a ship, there's usually some water as well*

"May I look too?"

Helmsman Odysseus Hirsch handed me his telescope. We were leaning on the *Liberty*'s rail, looking down. I always felt that the hour before the passengers came aboard was a very special time. Even up here, thirty or forty feet above their heads, the emotions of the people standing down there beside the ship—their hopes and fears—seemed almost tangible. Imminently prepared to venture into an unknown future and leave behind all that was familiar to them, no matter how unpleasant it might have been, those 179 emigrants from a dozen European countries possessed a powerful aura. Yes, it was a special occasion, although I must have witnessed it a hundred times.

"Thanks," I said, raising the telescope. The throng—despite the summer temperatures, most of the waiting figures were wearing winter overcoats or jackets and hats or caps—suddenly acquired individuality. Hugely magnified, their faces glided swiftly past me as I pivoted my head. Dangling in front of one of them was a little shoe. When I steadied the telescope, I made out a child sitting on a man's shoulders. I couldn't tell if it was a boy or a girl—its hair was hidden by a cap—but it was looking straight into my eyes. Then it said something to the man, who raised his head, and pointed to me with its arm outstretched. On impulse, I reached sideways, whipped the helmsman's cap off his head, and waved it in salutation. The child laughed.

"Hey, you crazy?" Odysseus snatched the cap back and replaced it on his bald pate. Then he spit his quid over the rail, relieved me of his telescope, and sauntered off. "I'm going."

Leaning over, I saw the milling crowd grow quiet. The quartermaster had stepped out onto the gangway and raised his arms in a mute request for silence. Standing there like a conductor, he launched into his little speech of welcome. It was July 12, 1879, and this was probably the last time I would hear it, for after this voyage in the *Liberty*, the fastest and biggest transatlantic sailing ship, I would transfer to something much faster and bigger still: my future workplace was to be the *Gigantic*, the superlative new oceangoing steamer that did the Hamburg–New York run in six days instead of sixty. I was already in possession of my contract as ship's hairdresser of the *Gigantic*, and I would board her in New York.

It so happened that the *Gigantic*, of all ships, was putting into Hamburg from New York on this of all days. I had already been able to smell her approach for several minutes. The strong westerly wind was propelling the yellowish-brown cloud that belched from her three smokestacks. Also audible now was the deep, hoarse note of her siren, which was quickly growing louder—very quickly, in fact, because it was already drowning out the quartermaster's words. Then the vessel itself appeared. Its sheer size was phenomenal. As it glided past the *Liberty*, its huge shadow engulfed the sailing ship and the quay on which the passengers were waiting to board.

"She's going far too fast," said Odysseus, who had suddenly reappeared beside me. "She shouldn't be, not here . . ." He was right, because the consequences could already be seen below us: the *Gigantic*'s wake was sucking the *Liberty* away from the quayside. The hawsers tautened, creaking like a hundred rusty barn doors. They held, but the wooden gangway on which the quartermaster was standing came adrift from its mountings and sagged into the abyss between the ship's side and the quay. Arms raised and mouth agape, the man disappeared from the passengers' view like an actor abruptly quitting the stage via a trapdoor.

"Damn it!" cried Odysseus. "He'll be crushed." He vaulted the rail and clambered down the iron ladder like a monkey. "Throw me a rope!" he yelled.

But it was already too late. I saw the water that had disappeared like magic suddenly flow back, forcing the *Liberty* against the quayside. It welled up fast, and the gap that had swallowed the quartermaster steadily narrowed. The full length of the ship's hull crashed against the quay. At the same moment—no, it must have been the bat of an eyelash before—the quartermaster came whirling up out of the abyss. For one brief moment, he hovered high above the passengers' heads; then his wriggling figure fell to earth in their midst. Momentarily transfixed, they came to life when the water, which had been forced into the air between the ship's hull and the quayside, descended on them like a fountain.

Almost any reaction would have been understandable, but this one surprised me: having formed a circle around the bemused quartermaster, who got up on all fours and then scrambled to his feet, the passengers applauded. Cries of "Bravo!" rang out.

I left the rail and set off for my cabin, which also functioned as my hairdressing salon, to make preparations for the evening. Some of the ladies were bound to want their hair done before appearing for dinner at the captain's table.

I was halfway there when the captain himself came hurrying toward me with his shirt hanging out and his suspenders trailing. He had been enjoying his last onshore nap, as he always did before we sailed. He caught me by the arm. "What happened?"

"Wherever there's a ship," I replied, "there's usually some water as well. The passengers know that now."

He stared at me with his little lashless eyes, under which huge pouches lay like protective sandbags. "In that case," he said, and turned on his heel.

The quartermaster, an old friend of mine, was in quite a bad way. He could easily have broken his neck on the stone quayside, but he'd been lucky to get away with a shattered shoulder, two dislocated arms, and a fractured tibia. His fall had been mitigated by the press of bodies into which he fell, which cushioned the impact.

I attended to him while we waited for the horse-drawn ambulance that would convey him to the harbor hospital nearby.

"Skrik," he said, breathing heavily and in obvious pain, "everything's all prepared. You can't go wrong." He asked me to take over the allocation of the passengers in his place. I was told to feel in his jacket pocket for the passenger list and the numbers of the cabins they had been assigned. "How do I look?"

"Wonderful."

"Sigismund—the truth, please."

It's always hard to tell a vain man the truth, so I said nothing.

He gingerly felt the congealed blood on his forehead. "Thanks," he whispered before he passed out.

I didn't have a list detailing the names of the others—the ones who would spend the voyage on the lower deck. The quartermaster called them *les misérables* when we were alone, not that he meant to demean them. No, he pitied those passengers who could only afford a berth below the waterline, and he had, in all the years we'd sailed the Atlantic together, done much to make their long weeks below more tolerable—and the *Liberty* could be at sea for as many as ten weeks if the wind dropped. He had, for instance, prevailed upon the captain to provide them with fresh water every other day instead of only once a week.

I watched the horse-drawn ambulance go jolting off with him in the back, then proceeded to usher the soaked passengers aboard. I was relieved not to have to go below and take over the distribution of bedding and eating utensils. The captain had summarily entrusted that task to the dark-skinned galley hands, whose appearance struck terror into the younger children. Their screams could not be heard for long, fortunately, because the hatches to the holds that housed the second-class passengers' bunks were swiftly closed.

But even up above in first class, getting the passengers installed was more of a commotion than usual. The question of where to put their sodden clothing presented the captain with a knotty problem. He eventually declared himself willing to place the sundeck at their disposal for drying clothes, with the result that gowns, petticoats, and silk stockings were fluttering beside the flags that adorned the *Liberty* when she sailed.

I studied the names on the list of upper-deck passengers. Only one of them was familiar to me: Bettina, Baroness von Reventlow, who often traveled aboard ships of the Hamburg-America Line, the *Liberty* included. I had made Betty's acquaintance years earlier in Boston, where I was acquiring my reputation as a high-society hairdresser, and where Betty was simultaneously becoming the favorite courtesan of nouveau riche American industrial tycoons. She had later, in return for a princely fee, taken to accompanying some of her admirers on their transatlantic voyages, which they undertook sometimes for business reasons and sometimes purely for pleasure. She was evidently returning alone from one such excursion, because no companion was listed.

Insistent cries could be heard outside my cabin. Then someone hammered on the door. I opened it with a beaming smile and invited my first lady customers to enter. There were seven of them. The contrast between their disheveled hair and their festive gowns, which they had already donned in preparation for dinner, could not have been greater. They exchanged suspicious glances as they lined up in front of me, then turned to me and all spoke at once.

I had encountered similar situations before, though they had involved only two or three customers, not seven, so I resorted to the same proven tactic this time: instead of debating whom to help first, I silently stationed myself beside the dressing table, picked up a comb in one hand, and gestured to the chair with the other: they were to agree on the order themselves.

Which they did. They eyed one another in silence at first, then the youngest of them stepped back. "After you," she said to the others. They shook their heads. "No, after you," said another. "No, no, after you!" "No, please go first," said a third and a fourth. This went on until the only one left was urged by the rest to go first. She was the eldest, a wrinkled little woman whose hair would have constituted a challenge for any hairdresser, even without that afternoon's shower bath. She surveyed the others with a gracious air, then came toward me and extended a begloved hand, which I took and conducted her to the chair. "I'm Countess Urbach," she said in an unexpectedly loud voice. "Delighted to meet you all."

That broke the spell. The other women crowded around her, talking volubly and introducing themselves. One of them pointed to the mirror on the dressing table and giggled. All seven leaned forward and stared at it, stunned by the sight that met their eyes. "Seven drowned kittens," said the countess. Tinkling laughter was the response.

They all watched me at work until the last of them was satisfied with her appearance. "Yes, it's really you," sighed Countess Urbach, giving me a look of gratitude, "the great Sigismund Skrik, master hairdresser of the seven seas. Who hasn't heard of you?"

"Of the Atlantic, only the Atlantic," I modestly corrected her. Looking up from my work, I saw another ten disheveled heads peering around the door to my cabin.

That was the moment when the *Liberty* sailed. First-class passengers normally spent it on the upper deck, quaffing champagne and listening to a brass band playing down on the quayside. This time it was different. The little jolt as the ship cast off, and her slight but unexpected list, sent a tidal wave of ladies surging out of the passage and into my cabin, where they reeled into those already there and knocked them over. Having steadied myself against the bulkhead, I stood like a victorious general amid the women lying at my feet.

# 2

# *That's what I really like about you—you never contradict me*

The atmosphere in the first-class dining saloon that evening was excellent, positively exuberant. One topic of conversation, of course, was the incident that had preceded boarding; another was the expert way in which the ship's hairdresser had refurbished the ladies. I wasn't present when that was discussed—the crew, of which I was privileged to count myself a member, took their meals in the mess beside the galley; only the captain and the first officer ate with the passengers—but the stewards hurried past me every time on their way from the saloon to the kitchen and vice versa. "The ladies are delighted!" the wine waiter called to me. "They call you a miracle worker."

I had indeed done good work. In short order and under adverse circumstances, I had succeeded in making them all look presentable and given them the feeling that they need never fear for their appearance on board this ship, whatever happened.

Betty came to see me later that evening. She had come aboard the *Liberty* at the last minute, after the geyser of seawater had already wrought havoc. She always came aboard like that: in a tearing hurry, one hand clutching her skirts, the other clamping her hat to her head.

She visited me when peace had descended. I recognized her by her perfume even before she entered my cabin. "I hear this is the last time we'll meet aboard this ship," she said, closing the door behind her. "So you're being unfaithful to me?"

"What's to prevent you from switching to the new steamer, like me?" I retorted.

"Money, perhaps? It'd be ten times as expensive. Unless I traveled second-class, but then I wouldn't be entitled to visit your salon." She came over to me and held out her hand, which I promptly put to my lips. "Don't worry," she said reassuringly. "I shall still be able to afford your services in the future. The last few months have been the most profitable of my life."

She seated herself at the dressing table. "Turn it down a bit," she said, indicating the kerosene lamp and looking at herself in the mirror. "I look awful—years older."

This was pure coquetry, but I forbore to contradict her and dimmed the light.

"That's what I like about you," she said. "You never contradict me."

"Hairdressers can do many things, but never that."

I had first met Betty in Boston fifteen years earlier. She was the daughter of poverty-stricken Baron von Reventlow, who had escaped his creditors by emigrating with his family from Hessen to America. He had invested his fortune in a lignite mine that proved to be unproductive. The Reventlows had done a moonlight flit and made the crossing in second class. The baroness, who contracted pneumonia on the voyage, later died of it. The baron cut a dashing figure in Boston society on the strength of his title and soon found himself harried by another bunch of angry creditors. He was said to have headed west one day, never to be seen again. His elder daughter went into a convent; Bettina, younger and prettier, found employment in the home of a charitable Polish count who was active in the railroad industry.

That was where I met her for the first time, when I was engaged for a ball at which the ladies' hair was to be styled *à la* Louis XIV. I originally took her for the count's granddaughter, but this assumption was dispelled at a late hour by the air of intimacy between them.

I had forgotten all about Betty when, some time later, I encountered her in quite similar circumstances at a summer party held by a Jewish banker. He introduced her to his guests as his daughter who had just arrived from Europe, and he held the party just for her. That evening she made the acquaintance of a number of influential male members of Boston society.

By the time we became really close, I was already plying my trade aboard ship, and she was accompanying a wealthy Englishman—he had made his fortune from cotton plantations in Louisiana—on a trip to Europe. And here I must qualify the word *close*: we never became physically intimate, although we were soon on familiar terms. During the conversations we had while I was doing her hair, we discovered that we were kindred spirits. When she described her most recent visit to her sister at the convent and said how revolted she was by her patent infatuation with the mother superior, I knew exactly what she meant. "She allows herself to be humiliated by that woman, yet she presumes to tell me how to lead a life pleasing to God."

"It's better to lead a life pleasing to man," I said approvingly. She stared at me in the mirror as if she had just undergone a revelation and asked me to address her by the familiar *Du* from then on.

. . .

Needless to say, she looked anything but awful that evening, and far from years older—a little more experienced, perhaps, and a trifle more attractive—but I didn't tell her so, just gently massaged her scalp in companionable silence. While the *Liberty* sailed slowly up the Elbe toward Cuxhaven and darkness spread its cloak over the waters, she recounted the latest episode in her story.

She had come straight to Hamburg from St. Petersburg, she said, having seen little of the place despite spending almost four months there. Her invitation to stay with Prince Abrassimov at his residence on the outskirts of the city had been transmitted by a woman friend who often worked in Russia. Betty did not discover that the prince was in his late seventies and bedridden until her arrival, which had been preceded by an arduous journey: the ship that should have brought her from Lübeck to St. Petersburg had been captured by Danish rebels and chained up in the Copenhagen harbor, so she spent the last stage of the journey in a one-horse carriage.

However, her arrival at the prince's palace compensated her for all these unpleasantnesses: awaiting her was an entourage of four lady's maids who pampered her like a child for the first few days. She didn't have to lift a finger and enjoyed several sumptuous meals a day, and it was a week before she set eyes on her host for the first time. The day before she received a visit from his sister, whose detailed explanation of what the prince expected of Betty was remarkably discreet but explicit.

The next day, having been carefully tutored in this way, she was ushered into the prince's bedchamber and left on her own with him. He was sitting up in bed in a nightshirt with his eyes shut, but she could tell he was only feigning sleep. She sat down on a chair and waited. He did not look as mortally ill as she had been given to believe, but she saw on closer inspection that his cheeks had been thickly rouged.

After a few minutes, while she was surveying the magnificent bedchamber, he opened his eyes and looked at her. "My child," he said, "how delighted I am that you should be visiting your old father in his sickbed. And that you're wearing the sailor suit I like so much." He put out a hand and drew her closer. "How good you smell too. Will you keep me company for a while?"

She was holding a book in her hand, a children's book she'd been given. "Yes," she said, "if you'll read to me. Will you?"

"Of course, my dear child. For as long as my strength holds out."

She sat down beside him on the bed and he read to her, holding her hand. After a few minutes he said, "My dear daughter, how inconsiderate of me. You must be freezing in that sailor suit! Come under the covers before you catch cold." Which she did.

Betty learned that the prince had no children. In the days that followed, he seemed to thrive on his new paternal role. Although he never quit his bed, he looked better from day to day. He allowed her to bring toys and dolls with her, and the lady's maids laid out a fresh costume for her before every visit. It turned out that he liked her best in a woolen romper suit, but it was so warm that she usually removed it before long. Then he would invite her under the covers to prevent her from catching a cold.

After two months, he even tolerated her presence in his bedchamber overnight—an unprecedented occurrence, according to his sister. One night Betty woke up shivering beneath the huge quilt. The prince's body was cold as ice.

To Betty's surprise, the person who turned up on the eve of her departure was not the prince's sister but a dignified gentleman, a notary. He informed her that the deceased had named her his sole heir a few days before his death. Apprised of this news a day earlier, the sister had promptly thrown herself out a window.

I massaged Betty's scalp a while longer, and she dozed off under my hands.

# 3

# *One of them will make it . . .*

The North Sea and the English Channel, so often the first ordeal undergone by passengers bound for America, allowed the *Liberty* to cross unscathed on this occasion. In glorious weather and under a full spread of canvas, we enjoyed the sight of England's green coasts gliding past on the horizon. They gave our passengers the feeling that they had not yet turned their backs on Europe finally and forever. Filled with zest and optimism, although there was really nothing for them to do, they engaged in animated discussions on the foredeck, struck up friendships, and discovered mutual acquaintances in the native lands they had left behind. Toward noon, they were served an aperitif in the saloon. The second-class passengers then had the deck to themselves for an hour, at liberty to inhale the fresh, salty sea air and have their hair ruffled by the wind. They couldn't stroll around like the others, of course; there were too many of them. Tightly packed together, many with children in their arms, they spent a while standing silently shoulder to shoulder before being shepherded back into the ship's dark maw, where they vegetated on their bunks by the light of kerosene lamps and waited for the next meal.

On the third day, the mood of the second-class passengers changed—very much for the better. The reason? A man who appeared on the passenger list as Dr. Heinrich Birnbaum, zoologist of Leipzig, had four macaque monkeys in packing cases right down below, where the ship's cook kept the pigs and poultry available to first-class passengers as fresh meat during the voyage. The airholes drilled into the cases appeared insufficient for the animals, so the zoologist had requested the captain's permission to release his charges on deck once a day. His request having been initially denied, a compromise was reached: one monkey a day would be allowed a brief spell of daylight at the hour when the deck was occupied by second-class passengers. The advent of these comical little animals proved a source of delight, especially to the children.

They clung to the zoologist with leashes around their necks, surveying the scene with darting eyes and occasionally baring their teeth in a way that suggested they were smiling at those around them. The passengers were particularly taken with Cora, the youngest of the four monkeys, all of which were female. Trembling all over but unresisting, she allowed the children to touch her and even, after a while, to tickle her little head. After a week, she became so accustomed to her new situation that Dr. Birnbaum put her down on the deck, took her paw, and promenaded among the passengers with her.

These were the mornings' highlights, and even first-class passengers thronged the windows of the saloon to watch the spectacle. However, Cora's popularity on board had an adverse effect on the other three macaques, which were seldom removed from their crates because everyone demanded to see their favorite monkey.

One afternoon—we had been at sea for a week, and the British Isles had disappeared below the horizon by now—Dr. Birnbaum appeared in my salon leading Cora by the paw. She was toddling along with one arm timidly covering her eyes. “Oh!” I exclaimed in surprise. “You’ve dressed her up.”

And indeed, the monkey was wearing a red skirt—not just a piece of material wound around its waist, but a regular skirt.

“I was positively compelled to,” said the zoologist. “It was a gift from one of the children. I was very touched. I accepted it, of course—who could have found it in his heart to refuse? And now we have to wear it, don’t we?” He stroked Cora’s head, whereupon she lowered her arm, made a sucking noise with her pursed lips, and looked up at him.

I was wondering what all this had to do with me when he went on, “I wouldn’t take it amiss if you refused my request, I assure you; in fact, I’d quite understand. You’re the ship’s hairdresser, the ladies’ most important figure in this closely confined community—I mean, what would your clientele think? On the other hand, they don’t have to know . . .”

“Know what?” I asked.

“Would you be willing to do Cora’s hair? It wouldn’t take long, and only in the mornings before I take her up to the foredeck.”

It surprised me to feel the silkiness of the fur covering the monkey’s pink scalp as it stood on my chair and bared its teeth at its reflection in the mirror.

“She’s unfamiliar with such things, perhaps . . .” said Birnbaum, indicating the mirror.

I draped a cloth over it, and the monkey calmed down. More than that, she grasped my hand and held it very tightly in her fingers. With my free hand, I took a soft brush and tried brushing her fur in one direction or the other, which proved a failure. I debated for a moment, then moistened my fingers with water and wound some of her head fur into a small ringlet. Picking up a length of red silk ribbon, I held it in front of the doctor. “Would you mind tying it around the ringlet?” I asked.

A few moments later, the monkey's head sported a bow that perfectly matched the color of her skirt. Dr. Birnbaum clapped his hands delightedly, with the result that Cora once more covered her eyes with her arm and let go of my hand. My fingers felt numb, the little creature had gripped them so tightly.

From now on, the hour between eleven and twelve became the highlight of the day. When Cora made her first appearance on the sundeck in her skirt and bow, the first-class passengers could restrain themselves no longer; they poured out of the saloon, thrust the children aside, and crowded around the zoologist and his monkey.

During their visits to my salon, which took place just before eleven every morning, I learned the reason for their journey. The macaque population had been decimated by a viral infection originating in the Asiatic rain forests, and zoos all over the world were endeavoring to prevent the extinction of this two-million-year-old species, which many people considered to be our ancestor. The Lincoln Park Zoo in Illinois owned one male specimen and the Dresden Zoo four females, so it had been agreed that the five animals should be brought together in hopes that they would breed. "And even if not all of my four ladies survive the journey, one of them will make it," said Dr. Birnbaum.

That one, alas, wasn't Cora, who went overboard on one of her morning outings. Dr. Birnbaum had unwisely taken to leading her around by a paw instead of on a leash. Suddenly snatching her paw away, she bounded over to the rail and perched on it. Then, raising one arm as if in farewell, she disappeared over the side.

# 4

# *So this is the boy wonder!*

Cora was not the first monkey I had encountered. My visits from Dr. Birnbaum and his charge had summoned up childhood memories of another equally small and equally comical monkey. I must have been around five years old and living with my parents on Herr von Wietersheim's farm in Westphalia—my father was a day laborer before he settled down with my mother—and I was already inured to hard work. As soon as I could walk, I was roped into all kinds of tasks on the farm: feeding the hens, gathering up straw that had fallen from the horse-drawn wagons, taking kitchen scraps to the pigs, and—my favorite occupation—filling the cats' wooden bowls with milk. Yes, I enjoyed all the chores I was given and loved the farmyard's noises and smells. I could hardly wait to leave our shack at dawn with my parents. My mother, a kitchen dairy maid, and my father, a farmhand who performed all the tasks that fell upon him, from chopping trees to slaughtering pigs, were my role models. They too could hardly wait to embark on their daily work.

What delighted me even more than the cats was the animal that accompanied the knife grinder on his infrequent but regular visits. I did not know at the time that it was a guenon—that is to say, a kind of monkey—but I have never forgotten its name: Bo. Bo sat on the handcart the man pushed ahead of him, which contained his whetstone and all sorts of utensils including brushes and combs, for he also worked as a barber.

Like all itinerants, he was barred from entering the house, so he stood at the window of the farm kitchen and was handed the knives to be sharpened. Standing beside him, I looked up at Bo, who sat on the edge of the handcart and assisted his master, whose name was Kröpelin. Bo passed him whatever he needed and cranked the handle of the whetstone against which Kröpelin held the blades as it gave off showers of sparks.

Neither of them paid me any attention until I had attained a height that enabled me to peer over the edge of the handcart, and one day, after finishing work, Kröpelin popped a candy in my mouth as well as Bo's. It was at about this time that the monkey also noticed my presence. Silently sucking our candies, we gazed into each other's eyes until the knife grinder went on his way.

When I grew older, it naturally didn't escape me what squalid conditions my parents lived in and how utterly at the mercy of the farm manager's whims they were, like all the other farmhands and menials. I cannot recall ever hearing them complain, however, and for some reason they seemed to be better treated than most of the others. There was much coming and going on the estate—someone was always being evicted for having stolen something, lied, or contradicted the master. By contrast, my parents and I continued to live undisturbed in our windowless shack year after year, and we were never accused of any misdemeanor. The farm manager occasionally beat us when some task had not been done satisfactorily, to be sure, but our livelihood was never seriously threatened.

This changed when my father accidentally fell into the well while drawing water, tore his leg on a piece of wood, and contracted blood poisoning. At first he was simply warned not to be off work for too long; then my mother became worried and summoned the doctor from the village. My father's leg had to be amputated above the knee.

My mother had bidden me to help her hold my father down on the floor—he had been drugged with a little camphor—while the doctor wielded the saw. I was strong and tall for a ten-year-old, and we managed to hold him still, for my mother was a sturdy woman whose daily butter churning had given her arms like steel cables.

From that day on, I knew that not even doctors can produce a sensible answer to every question. His work done, the man was about to leave our shack when my mother asked what was to be done with the severed leg, which was lying on the mud floor at our feet.

"Plant it in the orchard or give it to the pigs," he replied.

I don't think it was meant to be a joke, because he was eying us gravely.

"That's not funny!" my mother exclaimed, and she picked up the leg and chased him outside with it. We buried it near the stream that night at a spot of which my mother told me, "This, my son, is the place where your poor father and I first thought of you. You weren't born yet."

Father made a partial recovery, but work proved a problem. Not merely because most tasks were beyond him with a leg missing, but because he started drinking. It was my mother, of all people, who kept him supplied by bringing back beer from the kitchen. "I feel so sorry for him," she told me. "I simply can't bear to see him suffer."

The farm manager cut our rations—my parents were never paid in cash, only in board and lodging, and most of the food consisted of leftovers from the manor-house kitchen. In the past, these had been not only plentiful but very tasty. Now they weren't enough to feed the three of us. The more my father drank, the hungrier he became, so there were many days when nothing remained for my mother and me. She asked the manager to increase our rations, but he refused.

Then one day, Kröpelin turned up again. To my surprise, Bo was missing. He had died, I was told; monkeys didn't live forever. Kröpelin was obviously missing the animal's assistance. His work rate had slowed, and grinding all the knives was taking him longer than usual. As for cutting hair, he never got around to it.

Shortly before the end of the day, I saw my mother talking with him—something she had never done before. Having conversed at some length, they went over to our shack, where my father was lying on his mat, and spoke to him. Then they emerged and spoke with me.

The fact is, my parents had decided to sell me to Kröpelin. This would not only reduce the number of mouths in our shack, my mother explained, but provide money with which another, better, doctor could be summoned to treat my father's chronically inflamed stump. Otherwise his prospects would be poor. I could appreciate this, so that night I set off with Kröpelin in the role of his new assistant.

It would, of course, have been nicer had Bo been with us, but I had already ceased to miss the monkey much by the very next day, because the world to which Kröpelin introduced me was ample compensation. I, who had never before set foot outside the farm, was suddenly confronted with things that took my breath away: rivers, mountains, villages, towns, and people wearing costumes I had never seen before. And they all knew Kröpelin, all welcomed him and brought him their cutlery and tools. While I turned the spark-spewing crank, my master sharpened knives for all he was worth.

I also saw him trim a man's beard for the first time. I expected his customer to yell with pain at any moment, but he chatted happily with Kröpelin as if he couldn't feel a thing.

One night, when we had bedded down at a village inn where the landlord and his sons had had their hair cut by Kröpelin—we had been assigned two pallets in the henhouse—he said to me, "You'll do them in the future. I'm tired of messing around with people's lice-infested thatches." It was the first time he had addressed a complete sentence to me—he generally confined himself to single words like *knife*, *scissors*, or *whetstone* when he wanted me to pass them to him. "You've seen how it's done. Any fool can do it. Don't jab them with the scissors, that's all, or you'll be in for it."

The first of my "patients," as Kröpelin termed his customers, was a demented old man who lived in the attic of a house additionally occupied by his three sons—who jointly ran the family mill—together with their wives and a horde of children. The old man evidently owned the property, because he was treated with respect despite being quite insufferable. As soon as we entered the house, we heard shrill cries, crashes, and bangs coming from upstairs.

"Don't worry, you know what he's like," Kröpelin was assured by one of the women, who escorted us upstairs.

When she opened the door to the attic, I saw a bent-backed old man standing in the middle of the room surrounded by all manner of broken bits and pieces. He was trouserless. His emaciated body was clothed in a voluminous shirt that had presumably once been white but now matched the grayish-yellow shade of his skin.

When he noticed our presence, his face broke into a broad smile and his mouth opened to reveal a toothless cavity. He bowed to us in cavalier fashion, then swept an imaginary hat off his head. Long and abundant, his shaggy, matted hair stood out in all directions. "Is it time again," he asked in a high-pitched voice, "my dear Master Scissorman?" Then he flopped down in an armchair, leaned back, and waved his hand. "Ready when you are," he said, closing his eyes.

My master opened the leather bag of utensils, removed some scissors, and handed them to me. I took them and held out my other hand. "Brush and comb," I said. He passed them to me, and I took up my position behind the old man.

We left the house half an hour later, watched in silence by the three women, who were surrounded by a dozen of their children. Visible in the attic window was the figure of the old man, who kept running a hand over his head.

What had happened? I can only vaguely, foggily recall what went on in that upstairs room. As if in a dream, I began by softly and gently brushing the old man's hair, then slowly inserted the scissors. When the first strands of hair fell to the floor, I seemed to hear the impact as they landed on the floorboards, and the gloomy room seemed dazzlingly illuminated—yes, I experienced something akin to magic. Astonished, I saw myself carefully but purposefully cut and shape the old man's shock of hair. A creation came into being at my touch. My hands seemed to know what to do—I had only to leave them to it. The old man at first shut his eyes, but the tension in his body steadily subsided from minute to minute; he relaxed under my hands and obviously enjoyed what was being done to him. At some point he opened his eyes, put his head back, and gazed at me intently as I cut his hair. When the job was done and I returned the utensils to my master, silence reigned.

Word spread in the environs of Porta Westfalica, where Kröpelin plied his trade, that he was now accompanied by a young man, little more than a child, who was a superlative wielder of comb and scissors. A few weeks after our visit to the old miller's house, Kröpelin abandoned the whetstone and confined his business activities to haircutting alone. He was getting so many requests for haircuts, he could scarcely fulfill them all, with the result that people offered him a bonus if he could fit them in. It would be fair to say that the elderly hawker had suddenly become a made man. When we came to a town, he would set up his quarters at the inn in the marketplace, enter our customers' names on a list, and inform them of when their turn would come. We now paid house visits only to particularly wealthy customers or those unable to walk.

At the inns, barbering days became a kind of festive occasion. The taprooms thronged with those who had appointments and were killing time by drinking and playing cards, Kröpelin among them. The landlords paid him a fee for setting up shop in their establishments. I, on the other hand, noticed little of all this hurly-burly: I pursued my passion in a side room, performing one haircut after another. It was not long before I could scarcely recall having done anything else. More than one of my "patients" confessed that they had seldom felt as well as they did during those few minutes in my care. It wasn't just that the new haircut had made entirely new persons of them—the process itself was exhilarating.

Kröpelin adapted his appearance to his new reputation. He now wore silk knee breeches, linen shirts with wide sleeves, and buckled shoes of patent leather. And, because he knew to whom he owed his newfound prosperity, he provided me with a series of new garments. In Minden one day, I heard a woman passing by in the street remark that I looked like a young nobleman.

I can in all modesty say that I probably did cut a fairly presentable figure. This was the summer when my body sprung up: my shoulders grew broader and my legs longer, my round face developed a prominent chin, and my protruding ears surprised me by hugging my head more tightly. It was also the summer when I became acquainted with the first nobleman I'd ever met.

Count Hausendorf did not, of course, come to the inn—we were summoned to his castle as soon as we arrived in town. When we got there, we were kept waiting in the hallway for a while. Then the count suddenly appeared. "So this is the boy wonder!" he marveled. "Well, well."

It turned out that my patient was not the count himself—he wore a white powdered wig—but his five-year-old daughter, whose wealth of blond ringlets was to be tamed for the first time. The little girl was already seated on a table when we were conducted into her presence.

She was flanked by two sturdy maidservants, one of whom was draping a cloth around her scrawny shoulders.

We learned that several attempts to cut the child's hair had failed, purely and simply because she refused to cooperate. We were not informed exactly how she had resisted the barber's efforts, but I sensed on entering the room that this glowering tot would prove a challenge.

# 5

# *He wriggled like a stranded fish*

The sea became rougher when we left England behind and sailed out into the open Atlantic. The sky was usually gray and overcast, and spray came flying over the bow and onto the sundeck. The first-class passengers reduced their visits to the latter, but the passengers from "below" continued to come every day as a matter of course. Not only was their hour in the fresh air all too short, but their children were eager to see the monkeys.

Many of the passengers were now feeling sick. The ship's movements spoiled their appetite, and many of them preferred to spend the day lying down in their cabins, so peace descended on my salon after the hectic rush of the first few days. I enjoyed this, knowing that times would change.

Late one afternoon, when I rose from my chair after a brief nap, I received a visit from a young lady who hadn't favored me with her presence before. I strove to recall her name—after all, I had shown all the first-class passengers to their cabins on the day of our departure—but it eluded me.

"Don't worry, Master Skrik," she said, detecting my embarrassment, "I appear on the passenger list under a false name in any case." She left it at that and allowed me to conduct her to the chair.

She was a slim, dainty person with a translucent complexion and fine veins threading her temples. Her hands were as small as a child's. In stark contrast with her fragile appearance were her profuse auburn ringlets and her big green eyes, with which she regarded me in the mirror. It suddenly dawned on me who she was.

She wanted a haircut that would enable her to conceal her hair beneath a bonnet. "I know it'll be difficult, but we did it once before." She spoke as if it had been yesterday.

Yes, we had done it once before. My master, the count, and the two maidservants had watched me dubiously as I stationed myself in front of the little girl, Franziska von Hausendorf, who was seated on the table. "All of it!" ordered Count Hausendorf. "I want it all off! The stubborn brat must be taught that she can't flit around like a wood nymph." The maidservants were gripping the girl's arms as if to prevent her from rising into the air.

"Please leave us alone," I asked quietly. The count opened his mouth to object, but before he could utter a word, Franziska screamed. Not a very loud scream, but high-pitched and piercing. One of the maidservants clutched her ears, then everyone left the room. We were alone together.

"I want to do it myself," said the child, climbing down from the table and taking a pair of scissors from my leather bag.

"Without a mirror, you could hurt yourself."

Franziska considered this. "Sit down in front of me," she told me. I did so, and when our heads were on a level, she came right up close and looked at me. "I can see my reflection in your eyes," she said. Then she raised the scissors and applied them to her luxuriant ringlets. Within a few minutes, the little girl was standing in front of me not only shorn, but knee-deep in the fair hair that had fallen to the floor. "I'm sorry you have to go," said Franziska, and she picked up a ringlet and gave it to me. Then, going to the door, she went out and strode past those waiting outside without giving them so much as a glance.

This time, of course, I left her enough hair to form a coiffure that could be hidden under a bonnet if necessary. Then I opened the drawer of my hairdressing chest and took out a cardboard box. "Your hair has acquired a reddish tinge," I said, removing the blond ringlet and holding it up beside her head for comparison. She did not seem surprised that I still had it.

"Why are you here under an assumed name?"

"I ran away."

"From your father?"

"From my husband's family. I was betrothed to him shortly after you were summoned to the castle to cut my hair. He was five at the time. He hailed from a family that owned half of Westphalia and was on close terms with the elector. Our betrothal and the merger of our fathers' estates were intended to enhance their influence still further."

Franziska then told me where she had gone after leaving the room: straight to the stables, home of Raimund, the blacksmith's son, who was also five years old. She had promised to marry him, and he her. The children dreamed of a life on horseback far from the world of masters and servants. They hid in the hayloft from the count, who had followed his crop-headed daughter when she left the castle. She was naturally forbidden to play with servants' children, and naturally he found her doing so.

The blacksmith and his wife and children were banished from the estate, and Franziska was locked up in the cellar for a week with only bread and water. Thereafter she remained under house arrest until the day of her marriage, which took place on her sixth birthday.

From then on, she lived on her husband's estate. She hardly ever saw the boy, whose name was Ferdinand, because he underwent basic military training at a nearby barracks during the week and was instructed by private tutors when he came home on weekends. He developed into a strapping youth, whereas she steadily lost weight. She ate and drank almost nothing and seldom left her room. How to put an end to her miserable existence—that was her only thought.

And then, as she was looking out the window one day, she caught sight of Raimund: accompanied by his father the blacksmith, he was leading some horses across the courtyard. Franziska's spirits revived. She volunteered for tasks in the kitchen and herb garden in hopes of seeing Raimund, if only from afar. Eventually, when she asked her husband's permission to learn to ride and he granted her request, the time came: she entered the stable and promptly ran into Raimund, who seized her hand and drew her into a dark corner. They remained there the whole afternoon, locked in a tight embrace.

Franziska von Hausendorf, down on the passenger list as Claire Klüssendorf, hugged herself and closed her eyes.

"Where is Raimund now?" I asked.

"In America."

"Waiting for you there?"

She nodded.

"America is a big place."

She sighed.

"Does he know you're on the way?"

She shook her head.

"Were you followed?"

She shrugged.

"Is your hair short enough?"

She opened her eyes.

"What happened after you found him again?"

Nothing at all had happened at first, she said. She took riding lessons from Raimund's father, the young lovers went for brief outings on horseback, and her husband welcomed her activities and renewed *joie de vivre*. Raimund kept out of sight when her father came to visit, but that was all. Years went by in this way until, one day, her father turned up unannounced. She and Raimund emerged from the stable into the sunlight to find him standing there. "I might have known!" he shouted angrily.

Franziska escaped punishment, strangely enough, but Raimund was arrested on suspicion of taking fodder belonging to the estate and selling it to wagoners on his own behalf—a trumped-up charge, of course. In jail, he slept on straw in a damp cell he shared with vagrants, poachers, and potato thieves, some of whom had been waiting for years to be tried.

Franziska's husband never uttered a word about this. Instead he devoted all his time and energies to introducing his wife into society, for her sixteenth birthday was approaching and a big party had been planned. Tailors kept coming to fit and sew garments for her, and a fashion show was held where young society ladies modeled gowns for Franziska to choose from. Governesses were engaged to school her in polite conversation and dinner-table etiquette.

The only person through whom Franziska maintained contact with Raimund was Louise, Ferdinand's elder sister. No husband had yet been found for Louise, who was considered eccentric. She always wore black, conversed with trolls and elves when she walked on the grounds of the family estate, and insisted on taking leftover food to the prisoners in jail.

Franziska learned from her that Raimund was suffering from consumption. Louise offered to bring him medicinal herbs and letters but asked why Franziska's envelope was empty. Franziska explained that Raimund couldn't read, that it was merely meant to be a sign of life from her. On reflection, Louise advised her to sprinkle the envelope with perfume so he would know it was from her, which she did. From then on, Louise regularly brought her straws from Raimund's prison bedding—his way of responding to her "signs of life."

("I've filled a pillow with them," Franziska told me, "and it goes everywhere with me. It's in my cabin at this moment. In America, Raimund and I will lay our heads on it when we go to bed together.")

The closer the day of the birthday festivities drew, the harder it became for Franziska to pass Louise an envelope because she was so seldom left on her own. When a nun was engaged to instruct her in her forthcoming marital obligations, it became quite impossible. She was told that her sixteenth birthday would be the day on which her marriage would be consummated for the first time.

The nun was an amiable soul of indeterminate age—plump, short-winded, and apple-cheeked. She had no time for polite conversation but plenty for dialogues with God in which Franziska was also permitted to take part. When they sat together, the nun told God that her young charge would soon be dedicating her body to the fertility of His heavenly fields, that she would observe the Lord's commandments regarding the cohabitation of man and wife, and that she would bring her husband joy. And she asked God to give the young woman the strength to do this, eying Franziska with the inviting expression worn by adults when they promise a child an especially nice Christmas gift. She interspersed her lectures with hymns and always concluded them by giving Franziska a little present, sometimes a sprig of lavender or rosemary, sometimes a sachet of rose petals. These, she said, were to be placed under her mattress before her husband came to lie with her.

The festivities marking Franziska's sixteenth birthday consisted of an endless succession of meals. The guests arrived in the morning in time to partake of a substantial breakfast. Then came luncheon, followed by pastries and fruit in the garden at teatime. Meanwhile, in the great hall, preparations were being made for dinner, at which the main course would be trout from the estate's own fishponds.

Ferdinand did not leave Franziska's side. At dinner, they sat together at the head of the table, which seated fifty guests. Disaster struck when a guest raised his glass in a toast just as Ferdinand took a mouthful of fish. Ferdinand rose to his feet to respond to the toast and took a big swig from his glass. He was about to put it down when he froze, tilted his head back, and gasped for breath. His lips moved, but no sound emerged. His face turned puce and he flailed his arms, gripped his throat, and tried to retch. That too proved impossible—something had lodged in his gullet. After some seconds, his knees buckled and he slowly keeled over backward, upsetting his chair as he crashed to the floor.

He wriggled like a stranded fish while footmen thumped him hard on the back. Someone reached down his throat, but the fishbone was too deeply embedded. He was hurriedly carried out and taken to his bedchamber. There the poor youth's strength rapidly dwindled—he lay unmoving on the bed. Franziska entered the room just as the estate manager, a man of action, jumped on Ferdinand's chest with both feet. That did the trick. Ferdinand arched his body, and the morsel of trout went flying through the air. Then he sank back on the pillows, breathing harshly but alive.

He was bedridden from then on. Being deprived of air for such a long time seemed to have damaged a part of his brain, because he no longer spoke, no longer seemed to recognize anyone, and was incapable of doing the simplest things. He had to be washed and fed. Franziska volunteered to attend to his bodily needs, and the bedpan became her constant companion.

She almost forgot Raimund for a short time. Concern for her husband, whom she scarcely knew but whose condition profoundly distressed her, claimed her full attention. She now spent the night beside him in their marriage bed and watched for hours as his aimless gaze roamed the room. She could not catch his eye even when bending low over him.

It was Louise who brought Franziska back to life by informing her that Raimund would shortly be conveyed from prison into town because his trial was imminent. Filled with remorse, Franziska resumed sending her daily letters. And then, one morning, Raimund and the other inmates were brought out of the jail. They were a pitiful sight, those bowed, grimy, malodorous figures shuffling across the yard to the wagon in chains. But Raimund, or so it seemed to Franziska, was surrounded by an aura. While watching the procession with Louise from the prison gate, she got the impression that he glowed. He never took his eyes off her the whole time, and she knew that something was about to happen—something wonderful that would change her life.

Just as the wagon and its human freight emerged from the prison yard, the incident occurred. There was much speculation later as to what had caused it: either the fluttering habit of the nun, who was just coming down the road, or a sudden gust of wind. In any event, one of the horses shied, breaking the shaft and tipping the wagon into the ditch beside the road. The horses fell on top of the guards, and the prisoners tugged at their chains in an attempt to get out of the ditch, dragging each other down. Four were eventually fished out alive by peasants who hurried to the scene, but three drowned. Only one prisoner disappeared without a trace: Raimund.

It was a year before Franziska saw him again—a year in which she nearly went mad with despair and spent day and night beside her husband, who was becoming ever weaker. Late one night she was awakened by a noise and, looking up, saw Raimund standing beside the bed. She sprang straight into his arms. They stood there silently till dawn, clasping each other while her husband fought for breath. They would run away to America, Raimund whispered eventually—he would come for her tomorrow night, and she was to wait for him at the gate. Then he disappeared over the balcony just before the servants came in to give her husband his morning bath.

What happened the following night was her reason for sailing across the Atlantic on her own. She had gone to the main gate at midnight and waited. The utter silence that enveloped her and the infinity of darkness overhead had given her a taste of death, she said. She sensed that there was nothing between her and death: not God, not suffering, not happiness, just time. Time was the gift that death gave us, she told me: the gift of life.

Then Raimund suddenly came up behind her. The horses were saddled and waiting in the copse nearby, he said, but she replied that it wasn't yet time for her to leave. He must go on ahead by himself—her husband still needed her.

Raimund did not argue. Telling her that he would wait for her in America at the place where the ships put in, he disappeared into the darkness as noiselessly as he had come. As for Franziska, she went back and lay down beside her husband as he gasped for breath.

Ferdinand did not claim much more of her time. On the next moonless night, his labored breathing died away. After lying beside him for an hour, she went to the stable, saddled a horse, and set off on her journey to America. All she took with her was the generous dowry her father had provided, which still lay untouched in a carved wooden casket. Her husband had no more need of it.

Naturally, she attracted suspicious glances while making for the North Sea coast by way of Westphalia and Lower Saxony—she rode hell-for-leather, hoping to overtake Raimund—but people's curiosity was dispelled by the money that allowed her to spend the night in the best inns available. She took no special precautions until an incident at a tavern in Bielefeld, where she was assaulted by several young men who had been drinking. The landlord heard her screams and threatened them with a pitchfork, skewering one of them in the neck.

That night, Franziska took a pair of scissors and cropped her hair. Then she stole outside, purloined an armful of men's clothes from the washing line, and kept the garments that fit her. Leaving some money on the chest of drawers in her room, she quit Bielefeld at cockcrow. She attracted no attention from then on, especially as she now traveled by coach. She got to Hamburg in two weeks.

There she had to spend a year and a month before earning passage aboard the *Liberty*, forever in fear of bumping into someone who might have pursued her in order to bring her back. The money from her dowry had been just enough; now she was penniless.

When I asked why she had insisted on the *Liberty* when there were plenty of other vessels, she replied, "Because I would meet you on board." Although the ship had made several transatlantic trips in the meantime, she hadn't secured a cabin until now. She had seen posters featuring my name and picture, said Franziska. "You're famous," she told me as she rose from the chair and cast a final glance at her bobbed hair. "And to answer your question: Yes, I'm very satisfied."

It was true, I was something of a celebrity. In recent years, the agency that sold passages aboard the *Liberty* had taken to using my name in its advertisements. *Reach the New World Looking Chic, Courtesy of Master Skrik!* Posters bearing that slogan had been pasted up in the big waiting room of the emigration center at Hamburg's Overseas Quay, where the shipping lines had counters selling tickets. Although other transatlantic sailing ships now offered the services of a ship's hairdresser, I, being the first, was regarded as a pioneer. A caption beneath the slogan extolled me as "hairdresser to American high society." This was a gross exaggeration because my reputation was confined to Boston—elsewhere in America, I was as unknown as millions of other Germans. Nevertheless, it gave the ladies in first class the feeling that they were doing the right thing and entrusting themselves to the best of hands. The advertisement bore fruit: the *Liberty* was always booked solid.

I asked Franziska if she believed she was in danger of pursuers on board too. "If that were so," she said, "I hope you'd be the first to notice and warn me." She also thought it possible that someone might already be waiting to arrest her in America, which was why she intended to go ashore disguised as a man, a subterfuge that had stood her in good stead once before.

I promised to keep my eyes open.

Franziska's hairstyle became a topic of conversation on board. More than that, it became all the rage. The next morning, two ladies came and asked if it was true that her coiffure was the *dernier cri* in America. I said it was and added that, although it wasn't yet the prevailing trend, it would not be long before the most daring and attractive society ladies decided to wear their hair short. It was not only practical but expressive of a new, modern outlook on life—it set the seal, so to speak, on the obsolete conventions of the Old World.

In the days that followed, when more and more ladies came to me and requested the new hairstyle, I got the sneaking feeling that I might have cut off my nose to spite my face; the hairstyle was indeed so practical that the regular attentions of a hairdresser became unnecessary. Contrary to my fears, however, I did not run short of lady customers. They continued to come, claiming to need a shampoo when all they really wanted was a head massage.

# 6

# *Mother Superior of the Sacred Thornbush*

One day, during the third week of the voyage—the sea had subsided, and the sufferers from seasickness were reappearing on deck—my salon was visited by a woman I had scarcely noticed hitherto. She seldom flitted along the passageways and had her meals brought to her cabin. Although her clothing marked her as a nun, I was taken aback and rose reverently to my feet when she introduced herself as Mother Superior of the Sacred Thornbush.

I invited her to sit down at the dressing table, but she made a dismissive gesture. "I've nothing left to cut," she said, briefly removing her white cap to reveal a shorn head. "I'm here for quite another reason. You seem to be the only sensible member of the crew of this godforsaken ship." Her request was of quite a different order, she went on. She had already addressed it to the captain, but it had fallen on deaf ears.

She was concerned about the six young nuns with whom she was going to America to found a mission in Santa Fe, who were traveling second class. Although they were accustomed to spartan living conditions, the state of affairs down below was unacceptable. "Have you ever set foot in those sleeping quarters during the voyage?"

I said I hadn't.

"Nor has your captain. He refused to discuss them."

I knew, of course, that the converted cargo holds were cramped. The narrow, double-decker bunks were arrayed in long rows, one bed to each passenger.

"They sit there on their pallets by the light of kerosene lamps—men, women, and children—and scratch themselves to death amid the stench of the latrine buckets, which are emptied once a day. Those people need delousing—*you* must delouse them!"

She paced up and down in front of me, a short, energetic, middle-aged woman with her right fist driven into her left palm as if squashing a louse. Then she came to a halt and looked me belligerently in the eye. "What else are hairdressers for?"

I was about to retort that I could do little about the lice, even if I wanted to, because I didn't have enough ammonia with me—and anyway, it was the ship's doctor's job—but she was already rustling out of the cabin in her starched black habit. "I'm relying on you," she said without turning around.

I was naturally aware that unpleasant conditions prevailed below, just above the ship's keel, but lice were the least of the problems down there. Diseases—indeed, even epidemics and fatalities—were not uncommon during a voyage. Every member of the crew knew this, but they also knew it was those passengers who paid their wages because they cost almost nothing to transport. Second-class tickets might be cheap, but they made up a considerable proportion of a shipping line's revenues. First-class cabins, being expensive but few, were merely the icing on the cake.

That evening I passed Pablo, a galley hand, on his way down to second class and offered to help him carry one of the pails in which some thin, watery soup was sloshing around. Even as I descended into the bowels of the ship, my nose was stung by the evil stench rising from below. Pablo halted outside the door to the dormitory, reached into his trouser pocket, and removed two clothespins, sticking one on his nose and handing the other to me. I took it but did not put it on.

When he opened the door, some angelic singing came to our ears. "The nuns," Pablo explained.

I paused in the doorway, transfixed by the sight that met my eyes. Pablo deposited the soup pail in the aisle between the bunks and picked up the empty one from lunchtime, likewise the brimming latrine bucket. The first passengers came crawling out of their bunks and filled their bowls—each had been issued one—with soup. When Pablo passed me with the latrine bucket, I couldn't refrain from sticking the clothespin on my nose in double-quick time. He waited for me for a moment, but I stayed.

When my eyes had become accustomed to the dim lighting, I saw the six nuns. They were standing in line at the far end of the aisle, which was too narrow to accommodate them side by side, and their chorale was nearing its end. Several children were sitting on the deck in front of them, listening open-mouthed.

Silence fell when the last jubilant chord died away, broken only by the clatter of spoons on bowls. There was no reaction from anyone but the children, who eventually got to their feet, filled some bowls, and took them to the nuns. One of the latter pointed to me, whereupon a little girl proceeded to bring me some soup as well. Taking the bowl, I was surprised by the nasal voice in which I thanked the child. I had forgotten about the clothespin until she pointed to it. I quickly removed the clip and made her a present of it. Highly delighted, she ran over to the others. The clothespin was passed around and stuck on one little nose after another. The children's laughter sounded even lovelier than the nuns' singing.

Then I heard another soft but penetrating sound: people were scratching themselves, working on their heads and bodies with both hands. Many were scratching each other in places they were unable to reach themselves. I silently went to the door and slipped out.

In the passage leading to the companionway, I passed a storeroom from which issued the bleating of a goat. And a man's voice. Opening the door a crack, I saw Dr. Birnbaum, the zoologist, playing with his three remaining monkeys. He had released them from their crates, and they were happily clambering around on the shelves laden with stores. Now and again, one of them would sit still and wait for another to join it and inspect its fur, whereupon the latter would sometimes find something and quickly pop it into its mouth. I went in and closed the door behind me. An idea had occurred to me.

Dr. Birnbaum, surprised and pleased to see me, was quick to grasp my plan when I suggested it to him. It would be universally beneficial, he said. His monkeys were getting bored, and the second-class passengers were being tormented by vermin. The macaques had deloused only their own kind before, but it was worth a try.

The experiment proved a total success! A week later, when the mother superior revisited my salon, she could hardly find the words to express her gratitude. "You . . . you're a . . . a cunning devil," she blurted out. Then, realizing what she'd just said, she hastily crossed herself three times. "Mind you, I don't wish to know how you managed it." She never found out. Although news travels fast on a ship, especially a small one, it remained a secret between me, Dr. Birnbaum, the monkeys, and the second-class passengers.

# 7

## *She's never sung like that before!*

Toward the end of the third week of the voyage, we were nearing the seventeenth degree of longitude—the magical zone, as Odysseus Hirsch called it. The helmsman once told me that it was the only reason why he still went to sea. He could have retired, and possibly should have done so long ago, because his sight had been considerably impaired by looking at the sun through a sextant. Sometimes at the end of the day, when the sun had already set, it still seemed to be shining in his face, and it dazzled him even in his bunk at night. But he endured this because of the seventeenth degree of longitude and what awaited him there.

He had told me on the morning of the day in question that we would, at twilight, reach the area through which vast herds of sperm whales passed from north to south on the way to their grazing grounds off South America. Late that afternoon, when the last customer had left my salon, I went to the wheelhouse: a low, cramped shack from which the helmsman was looking ahead through a salt-encrusted window, his huge hands keeping a viselike grip on the wooden wheel.

The sea was mirror-smooth, and we were making good progress thanks to a gentle following breeze. The first graybacks and their intermittent fountains of spray could already be seen on the horizon, but Odysseus told me that it would be several hours before She appeared.

Even though, unlike him, I was unconvinced that She was the reincarnation of a Siren, there could be no doubt that She was a whale unlike any other. We had observed hundreds of those giants around our ship over the years, always new and different ones, but She reappeared every time. Seemingly at home in these waters, She guided the herds passing through. She knew when they would come, waited for them, and escorted them through the currents that crossed here. And She seemed to be waiting for him, Odysseus Hirsch.

Needless to say, the deck soon became crowded with passengers when word of the whales' appearance spread—and they were not disappointed. The animals escorted the *Liberty* for a while, dove beneath her, and leaped out of the water, grunting like aurochs. Delighted cries rang out when a cow showed off her calf to us by taking it on her broad back and circling the ship twice.

Odysseus had no eyes for this. Intently scanning the horizon through his telescope, he asked me to take the wheel—the highest honor he could bestow. Then he said softly, "There She is." At that moment, the ship's bell summoned the first-class passengers to dinner. "Just in time," said Odysseus. "Tie me up."

When the last passenger had left the deck, we hurried to the mainmast, where Odysseus had made all the requisite preparations. A stout rope lay ready for me to lash him to the mast, winding it several times around his midriff. Then I hurried back to the wheelhouse and took the wheel again. The sun was nearing the skyline, the water was tinged with red, and gliding toward us close beneath the surface was Her immense silver back.

I cannot deny that I was always profoundly moved by the spectacle that ensued. When She reached the *Liberty*—and I swear that She was almost as long as the ship herself—She raised her head above the surface and scanned the deck with her little eyes. When She sighted Odysseus lashed to the mast, she uttered a sound that pierced me to the marrow. It was the cry of a woman in love, but a hundred times louder—it must have been audible for miles. Then She dove for several minutes.

When She reappeared, close beneath the surface to port of us, and glided along beside the *Liberty*, She started to sing. The notes She emitted were otherworldly, high and low, loud and soft, long and short, at once harsh and gentle—notes that might have issued from a mighty church organ with all the stops pulled out at once. Odysseus writhed in his bonds and joined in. He tossed his head to and fro, and his voice became vibrant and ecstatic as it sought to match hers and join in her song, becoming another organ stop. He trembled all over, seeming to try to find a note that would merge with hers. And then She raised her enormous head out of the water, higher and higher, and thrust it over the rail until it nearly reached the mast where Odysseus was tugging at his bonds.

The final harmony felt never-ending. What terminated it was a dazzling shaft of lightning that issued from a solitary cloud in the otherwise cloudless evening sky and struck the sea. Her head loomed over Odysseus for another few seconds; then She slid back into the water, firing a fountain of spray into the air.

Having given Odysseus a few moments before untying him, I held him up in both arms to prevent him from slumping to the deck. Glassy-eyed and breathing heavily, he allowed me to lead him back to the wheelhouse. We stood there side by side watching the sun, which seemed to want to linger a moment before sinking below the horizon, and the red surface quickly turned pitch-black. She was nowhere to be seen.

"Please go now, Skrik," Odysseus told me, lighting a cigarette. He was streaming with sweat and still slightly tremulous. Emanating from the saloon were strains from the out-of-tune piano; a concert pianist from Moscow, who was on his way to California to make his fortune panning for gold, played for dancing every evening.

# 8

## *I'm the only person in the world who can tell*

I left Odysseus Hirsch and followed the strains of the piano into the saloon. No one there seemed to have any inkling of the sensational happenings outside; they were all clustered around a table with a deck of cards on it. All eyes were on the Urs Hütterlis, a couple from Zurich who had just been living in Baden-Baden, as I knew from the passenger list. They were the most glamorous spectacle on board: she tall and full-bosomed, positively majestic, with pinned-up blond hair; he even taller, broad-chested, broad-shouldered, and endowed with two rows of snow-white teeth, unveiled in every one of his infectious smiles.

Urs Hütterli, presiding at the head of the table, shuffled the cards with the onlookers crowding around him. His wife, Rosalie, one of the few women on the ship who hadn't subscribed to the new hairdressing vogue, was standing a little apart, watching the proceedings. The cards were fanned out on the table. "If you would care to draw a card, madam," Hütterli said to one of the ladies. "And now please replace it in the deck wherever you like." Again the sound of shuffling. The process was repeated, this time with a gentleman's assistance. When this had happened five times in all, Hütterli said, "Now please deal out the top five cards face up." When he asked if they were the cards that had been drawn, his question was answered in the affirmative. Cries of "Bravo!" and "Encore!" rang out.

Hütterli, never one to need asking twice, proceeded to perform his next card trick. As the spectators leaned forward intently, craning their necks, Rosalie Hütterli slowly approached and stationed herself just behind one of the male passengers. When the suspense culminated in loud applause, her hand shot out. After reaching into the man's hip pocket, she swiftly withdrew it—along with his wallet, which she slipped into her décolletage.

More cries of "Encore!" and yet another trick. Rosalie Hütterli circled the group, took up her position on the other side, and prepared to strike again. As she did so, our eyes met. She froze for a moment and stood motionless until her husband called out, "I must now enlist my wife's assistance."

She went and stood beside him with a radiant smile. I left the saloon.

The next morning, Rosalie Hütterli was standing outside my cabin when I opened the door. I invited her in, and she sat down without a word. Her hair was disheveled, her eyes red-rimmed.

Wearily regarding me in the mirror, she said, "You can see for yourself . . ."

I picked up my brush and comb.

Rosalie preserved a long silence while I did her hair. She gazed at herself in the mirror, lost in thought, and closed her eyes from time to time. As I gently massaged her scalp, she told me her story.

Her father had been a croupier in Montreux, Switzerland, and she had been attracted to the casino from a young age. Together with her mother, she had accompanied him to his place of work every evening.

They used to stand outside the snow-white building for ages, watching carriages drive up and dapper gentlemen in white scarves, gloves, and top hats alight with elegant young women on their arms—young women who threw back their heads and laughed, displaying their dazzling white teeth. Determined to be part of that wonderful world someday, Rosalie soon took to brushing her own teeth thoroughly before bed.

Her mother died giving birth to her second child, and her father employed someone to look after Rosalie while he was on duty. This woman, who worked the day shift at the casino as a cocktail waitress, patiently answered all her young charge's questions. When Rosalie lay in her cot and listened to her stories, her ears were filled with the rattle of roulette wheels, the hubbub of voices, and the clink of glasses; her nose with the scent of cigar smoke.

She wasn't sure if her father was having an affair with the babysitter, she said. It didn't matter to her anyway, because she had become very attached to the woman, whose name was Madeleine. It was also Madeleine who, when Rosalie turned eighteen, enabled her to enter the world of the casino by getting her a position as a part-time cocktail waitress. Her job was to clear away the glasses the customers left all over the place, even in the restrooms. This meant that she was constantly on the move in all parts of the casino, and she greedily absorbed everything she saw. She was happy. The customers seemed to her to be so carefree, so beautiful and invulnerable. Her eyes sometimes welled up with pride when she watched her father presiding over his own roulette wheel as *chef de table* and saw how elegantly he slid the chips to and fro, thanked some customer or other with a charming smile, and, with a self-assured gesture, pocketed a gratuity. He made the customers feel that it was an honor and privilege to play at his table.

And then, one night, she saw Urs Hütterli. He was seated at the far end of her father's table, and he looked like a man at work—in contrast with the other players, who were there for their own amusement, laughed uproariously, and, when they won, ordered champagne and shook hands all around.

Although Urs was generous when a stack of chips slid in his direction—in fact, he tipped the croupier even more generously than most—his thoughts were already on the next spin of the wheel. He was utterly focused, and his beautiful brown eyes—the first thing Rosalie noticed about him—were fixed on the ivory ball. He placed his bet as late as possible before it came to rest, and he often won. Very often. He always played at her father's table, always came on his own, and nearly always left the casino with more chips than he'd bought. He came every night for a whole winter, but one day he wasn't there anymore. That was the day her father was given notice—or, to be more precise, given an envelope bulging with cash and an injunction to leave town forthwith. The casino was anxious to proceed as discreetly as possible, because the last thing it needed was a rumor that one of its croupiers had been in league with a professional gambler.

Rosalie wasn't shocked in the least that her father was a swindler, nor that Urs Hütterli was a cheat. In her eyes, it only made him more interesting and desirable.

Yes, she had fallen for him on sight, she told me as I gently massaged her behind the ears. Just as she had known, even as a little girl, that she would someday work in a casino, so she had known at once that she would someday belong to Urs.

Her father told her that no casino in Europe would employ him from now on—that went without saying—but that Urs would continue to try his luck at the gaming table. When he further informed her that Urs intended to go to Monte Carlo, Rosalie quit her job in Montreux and applied for one in Monaco, where she was soon engaged as a cocktail waitress.

She glanced at me in the mirror. "I may not look it now, but I was a beauty in those days. I put most of the female gamblers in the shade." When she started work in Monte Carlo, Urs was seated at the roulette table as usual, facing the croupier and staring straight ahead. He appeared to have noticed her, however, because when he got up to cash in his chips after several hours, he briefly waited until their paths crossed. "I'm staying at the Palace Hotel," he told her.

They remained in Monte Carlo for two years. This time Urs stopped working at the casino before he and the croupier could arouse suspicion. He had made enough to treat Rosalie to a honeymoon in Marrakech, but they retained their hotel suite as a base for extended visits to major cities. Istanbul and Vienna were particular favorites of theirs. Germany was the only country omitted from their itinerary, but after two years Urs told her that his next port of call would be Baden-Baden. It was time for him to start work again, he said. Nobody knew him in the casino there, which was an advantage.

"Did you learn how your father and your husband worked together—I mean, what their system was?" I asked.

"No. I never asked Urs about it, and I haven't seen my father since he left Montreux. We received a letter from him shortly before we moved to Germany. From America. He sent his love to me, but the rest of the letter was addressed to Urs—on business, as he put it. He said there were undreamed-of opportunities for them both in America. First on the agenda, though, would be Baden-Baden. I would like it there, he said."

"And did you?"

"Very much. The casino is the nicest in Europe. It's paradise."

She was no longer working as a cocktail waitress, of course. She accompanied Urs as his wife, night after night, and relished the feeling that she belonged at last—that she was a member of that special breed to which she had always felt drawn. While Urs sat at the roulette table, she roamed the magnificent gaming rooms in a kind of dream and discovered the pleasures of gambling for herself. Her passions were craps and poker—and the wallets of men who, without turning a hair, won fortunes or gambled them away. The first wallet she took positively asked to be stolen: it was protruding from a gambler's hip pocket and in danger of falling out. In the ladies' restroom, she removed the bills and surreptitiously dumped everything else in the trash. Then she sat down at the craps table and placed her stake. She won nothing that night except the knowledge that she had made a new and wonderful discovery.

"Do you know how you can tell where a man's wallet is?"

"I don't even know where mine is," I said, patting my hip pocket.

"In the left-hand breast pocket of your jacket," Rosalie Hütterli said with a laugh, her lovely eyes shining. "It's only a fraction of a millimeter, but every man carrying a wallet involuntarily leans in that direction as if something is weighing him down. I can tell, and I think I'm the only person in the world who can."

"Were you always successful?"

"Twice I was too slow. The owners of the wallets noticed their loss before I could stow them away in my purse. I still had them in my hand."

Seeing me look aghast, she added, "Both times they thanked me for my honesty. 'What luck you were standing behind me,' they said, and invited me to share a bottle of champagne with them."

"And your husband?"

"He was pleased I was so successful at craps. Many nights, I brought home more money than he did."

I could tell that this was not the whole story. She thought for a while with her head to one side, and I massaged her some more.

There was this house detective, she went on. One night as she was emerging from the ladies' restroom, where she had just dumped a billfold, he asked her to come with him; he had something to show her, he said. He escorted her to the office, where he opened a closet. Neatly stacked inside were dozens of wallets and billfolds. They don't just dissolve into thin air, he told her—all the rooms are thoroughly cleaned and the trash cans emptied every morning. The cleaners hadn't thought twice about it at first, but when more and more men's wallets turned up in the ladies' restroom, they reported the matter to him.

"What made him pick on you?"

She didn't know, she said, but she'd made no attempt to deny the charge; in fact, she'd said nothing at all. Neither had the detective. He dropped the subject and wished her a pleasant evening.

But the very next night, he appeared at her craps table and discreetly drew her attention to a man who was making for the cashier's cage with a big stack of chips. Rosalie was able to relieve him of his wallet soon afterward. It had in fact been particularly easy, she added, because he left it on a table while paying at the bar and in conversation with another man.

The detective intercepted Rosalie on her way to the restroom. He neither threatened nor even spoke to her, but she knew what she had to do: she gave him the wallet, and he kissed her hand.

Strangely enough, this changed situation did not detract from her love of gambling. Urs, who was also enjoying Baden-Baden, made more there in a few months than he had in two years at Monte Carlo. She didn't know which croupiers he was working with, but he seemed to have refined his system still further. He told her that, although it was clear the casino management would have liked to send him packing because of all his winnings, they had nothing on him. Just another few months, he promised, and off to America they would go.

His gambling coups had not, of course, escaped the house detective's notice, and there came a night when he drew Rosalie's attention to her husband, who had just cashed in his chips. Stealing his billfold was only too easy because she knew exactly where he kept it. She abstracted it while they were standing together at the bar, enjoying one for the road. What was more difficult was to pass the billfold to the detective because Urs was still at her side, so she had to fall back on the proven restroom method.

Urs didn't notice his missing billfold until they were back in their hotel suite and he wanted to add his winnings to those already in the safe. She was sure he had only mislaid it, Rosalie told him soothingly; it would be found and returned to him tomorrow night without fail. But Urs mutely shook his head, convinced that he had been the victim of a pickpocket. He had never lost anything before, he said, it just didn't happen. True, he tended to be untidy and occasionally had to spend a long time looking for things, but losing his billfold—no, it was out of the question.

He sat down on the edge of the bed, buried his face in his hands, and wept. When he had calmed down, he told her that their only possible course of action was to leave at once. He couldn't go on living in such a corrupt and degenerate country—had no wish to breathe its deceitful, duplicitous air any longer. He had a lot of sympathy for human frailty and foolishness, but picking pockets was unforgivable—incompatible with the dignity he expected of life. "America!" he cried, folding Rosalie in his arms. "We'll be happy there."

When she had finished her story, Rosalie opened her purse and deposited two wallets on my dressing table. "Can you help me?" she asked. "My husband must never find out."

Returning the wallets to their owners was a relatively uncomplicated matter. I called on them in their cabins that evening and told them that the items had been found in the saloon. They had evidently fallen out of their pockets and slid beneath the table when the *Liberty* gave a lurch, struck by that sudden squall late last night. Both men remarked that they couldn't remember any such squall. No wonder, I told them, considering they were watching the card tricks so intently. Whereupon they thanked me, asked me to give the finders a suitable reward, and pressed some money into my hand on the spot.

# 9
## *Dreams in which I'm all feet*

Count Hausendorf must have paid a substantial sum to have his five-year-old daughter's head shorn. Master Kröpelin did not tell me how much, but the very next day he purchased a brand-new set of scissors, brushes, and combs. From now on, he explained, we would be moving in circles in which our rusty old equipment would be inappropriate. Kröpelin had acquired a well-chosen vocabulary as well as a new wardrobe. Henceforward, he declared, no doors would be closed to us.

Not long afterward, he bought a horse and carriage to replace the handcart with which he had toured the countryside for decades. The horse was old and inexpensive, but willing and easy to handle. Kröpelin knew nothing about horses, so it fell to me to look after the animal and drive the carriage. My master lolled under the canopy and dozed while I sat on the box and guided the horse. The animal's good points were offset by a certain lack of stamina, which meant that it had to rest at least every two hours—otherwise it simply stopped in its tracks. Since the swaying of the carriage usually sent Kröpelin into a deep sleep, he was unworried by this. So was I, who took advantage of these interruptions to perfect my technique. For this, I employed the tussocks of grass beside the road. The longer and shaggier they were, the more I liked them. I dug them up, put them on the box, and proceeded to trim and shape them with my new scissors. By the end of our interludes, which the horse signaled by ambling on, I would sometimes be surrounded by as many as half a dozen tussocks trimmed into the most fanciful hairstyles imaginable.

Among the regular ports of call on our travels were numerous army barracks whose occupants had known my master for years and made a habit of employing his services. "You'll do it in your sleep," he assured me as we trundled through the big iron gates of a hussar regiment's barracks, the first of many I would become acquainted with. "Soldiers' hair is easy to cut."

It wasn't the rank and file—they cut their own hair—but the officers who required the attentions of a barber. They all affected the same haircut, so I could have made things easy for myself. At first I did so, well aware that they were eying me warily and I couldn't afford to indulge in any extravagant flights of fancy. Their mistrust was soon dispelled, however, because I fulfilled their expectations and earned their praise.

This encouraged me. The first man in whose case I deviated from the standard officer's haircut was a colonel with a veritable bullet head: a broad forehead surmounted by a flat, rectangular cranium that fell away as steeply behind as it did in front. He looked like a rough-hewn boulder as he sat down in the chair. By the time I had completed my work and he was standing in front of the mirror, he resembled a Greek god. I had evened out all that was angular and abrupt about his appearance by leaving the hair alone in the right places instead of cutting it off, and, in others, carefully removing just enough to endow the head with entirely new proportions.

The colonel slowly turned to me after inspecting himself in the mirror. "How did you do that?" he demanded, staring at me. "Was it witchcraft?"

Master Kröpelin, who had been dozing on a chair in the background, awoke with a start and hurried over to our intimidating client. "We can do it again, sir—we can do it just the way you want it," he said hastily.

The colonel thrust my employer aside with one hand and, never taking his eyes off me, said, "You weren't trained by this cretin, were you?" Going right up to me and bending down, he put a finger under my chin and tilted my face toward his. "You're an artist."

In the years that followed, the members of the Westphalian officer corps became immensely popular with the ladies. I wouldn't presume to claim that this was all my doing, but other people thought so, and I now believe there must have been a smidgen of truth in it, because the barracks all competed for our services, and Master Kröpelin's order book was full six months in advance. Agreeable though this was, its disadvantage was that we could no longer traverse the countryside at our own leisurely pace, as dictated by our old nag, but had to be in certain places on certain days.

I don't know whether Kröpelin realized that our universally good reputation owed little to him. Now that business was flourishing, he had taken to opening his first bottle of rotgut in the morning and spent the rest of the day in the carriage. He was more and more often incapable of dealing with army officers and arranging new appointments with them, so that task devolved upon me too. I wasn't worried, though, because my master was so seldom seen that he didn't attract unwelcome attention.

But there came a time when this worked to his disadvantage. At the end of one busy day in a barracks near Münster, where I had cut more than twenty officers' hair, I was summoned to see the commandant, a gray-haired, amiable-looking old general. Without ado, he said,

"Your master will be leaving without you. From now on, you'll remain at our service. You'll get board and lodging and a fixed salary. And a room in which to ply your trade."

"What about my master?"

"Who needs him? He's history. He can console himself with that stock of liquor in his carriage."

Kröpelin had left the barracks by the time I emerged from the general's office.

Over the next few weeks, I gradually discovered the reason for my abduction: a veritable war had broken out between the various regiments competing for my services. They had outbid each other in an attempt to gain Kröpelin's favor, so he must have wound up a wealthy man. The general had now killed two birds with one stone: his regiment not only had me to itself—standard haircuts would once more be the rule in other barracks—but it had acquired my services considerably more cheaply than before.

I enjoyed life in the barracks. My days began early and ended late. I got little sleep, but that didn't bother me. I was at an age when, although life seems eternal, one wants to savor every minute of it, so sleep is only a hindrance. As the commandant had promised, I had been assigned a bedroom with my very first bed of my own, plus a chair, table, and closet, and a separate room in which to work. Affixed to the door was a brass plate inscribed "Barber."

The commandant strode in one morning, sat down in the chair, put his head back, shut his eyes, and said, "Shave."

This was a novelty. Kröpelin had continued to trim our customers' beards to the last, even after I had gained a reputation as a hairdresser. But my spell of confusion lasted only a moment or two; then I was overcome by joyful excitement. The commandant sported a mustache whose ends curved upward about an inch to the left and right of his nose. His chin, neck, and cheeks were clean-shaven, but now, early in the morning, they were frosted with the sprinkling of bristles that had grown overnight. I draped a towel around his neck, lathered his face with soap, and proceeded to shave him. In the meantime, I studied his mustache.

I soon grasped what had to be done. Taking my finest scissors, I snipped a few millimeters off his mustache here and there until it was completely even, then took a small, round brush, applied it to the tapering ends, and very gently curled these inward. I held them like that for several minutes, then curled them a bit more. I repeated this process several times until the ends of the mustache curled inward like snail shells. The commandant had opened his eyes while I was doing this, and was regarding me intently. He must have been puzzled, but he asked no questions. When I returned his gaze, I was struck by his luxuriant, bushy eyebrows, which stuck out all over the place. Carefully removing the little brush from his mustache, I applied it to his eyebrows and curled their ends into tiny spirals, not only either side but in the middle, over the bridge of his nose, where the eyebrows almost met. These also retained their shape when I finally removed the brush.

Then I stepped back and inspected my work. I wished his mustache had been a bit longer, so that I could have made the snail shells more impressive, and I resolved to achieve this by degrees on future occasions. He slowly removed his eyes from mine and turned to face the mirror, which was only a shard the size of a man's palm. He peered at it in silence, bending forward until his nose touched the glass. Then he looked at me once more. "You're worth your pay," he said, and got to his feet.

Three officers presented themselves for a shave the next morning. "Like the commandant!" the first bade me as he sat down in the chair, and the other two followed suit. Over the next few days, every member of the officer corps had his mustache and eyebrows styled like the commandant's.

This was a period when my creativity seemed to have no bounds. The officers' custom wasn't enough for me. In the afternoons, when the troopers rode out on exercises, I dug up tussocks in the neighboring cow pastures and styled them in a quiet corner of the barrack square. After some weeks, there was a whole row of my creations on top of a wall there. Many officers took to "reviewing" the tussocks with me. They would then point to one they particularly liked and simply say, "Like that."

One day, the commandant's wife put in a surprise appearance—accompanied by her husband, of course, because wives lived in the nearby garrison town and were not really allowed in the barracks—and convinced him to show her my collection. After that, more and more carriages came to call, with officers' wives alighting from them. When these comings and goings began to disrupt barracks routine, one Sunday was set aside for an official show to which local dignitaries and their female companions were also invited. Drinks were served, followed by a viewing of the exhibits, which had been transferred to the indoor riding arena and displayed on small tables especially for the occasion. They had greatly increased in number by now, so the guests took a long time to view them all.

I can justifiably say that that day proved to be a watershed in my career. Having hitherto cut only men's hair, I now acquired a wider sphere of activity. My first female customer was the commandant's wife, who sent word that she wished to see me.

Her name was Lydia zu Bärenbaum, née Kreyenfels. An unremarkable-looking woman of around forty, she was at least a head shorter than her husband, General Hasso zu Bärenbaum, yet one got the impression, when seeing them together, that he looked up to her. He really did, as I discovered on the morning of the appointment, when he summoned me for a lecture on how to behave during my encounter with his wife.

"I won't give you any instructions, my wife doesn't need me to," he began, "but get this into your head: my wife detests sentences that begin with the word 'I'—unless, of course, they're uttered by herself

Consequently, if you address a remark to her, which is advisable only if she requests you to do so, avoid that at all costs. Substitute 'Yours truly' or 'My mother's son' or 'The hairdresser present,' or anything else that occurs to you. Next, never look her in the eye, least of all if she says, 'Look at me!' Look instead at her feet, or at most at her knees. Again, don't wear bright colors—wear a sober jacket, preferably a gray one. My aide-de-camp can provide you with one if you don't own one yourself. Most important of all, no physical contact. Keep an appropriate distance between you—an arm's length at least."

He had been standing at the window during this homily, looking out at the barrack square, where recruits were practicing the regulation salute. Now he turned to me and asked, "Have you got all that?"

"Yes, sir."

"Any questions?"

"Er, yes, sir."

"Well?"

"How am I to do her hair?"

"Whose hair?"

"Your wife's."

"Who's the hairdresser here, me or you? Think of something, something out of the ordinary. My wife likes unusual things; that's why she asked for you."

"I meant, sir, how am I to . . . if I'm not allowed to . . . ?"

"That's all. Dismissed!"

Two hours later, I was standing outside the massive portal of the house where the general's wife lived. An aide had brought various jackets and trousers for me to try on before driving me to see her in a one-horse carriage. A maidservant answered the door and showed me into the drawing room. I had brought the leather bag containing my equipment, plus a wooden pole to which comb, scissors, and brushes could be attached, enabling me to do Frau zu Bärenbaum's hair without venturing within an arm's length of her.

For a while I stood there as silent as the room itself, where every sound was muffled by thick carpets and heavy, upholstered furniture, and waited for my client to appear. But she was already there, as I realized when a voice issued from a wing chair facing the big window with its high back toward me. "Cat got your tongue?" it said.

Not knowing whether to construe this as a request to speak, I decided not to reply for safety's sake. "Give me a refill!" the voice demanded.

I circled the armchair. She was sitting there with an empty wineglass in her hand, which she extended in my direction. I refilled it with wine from a decanter on the table in front of her. She took a long pull, then asked, "Why are you staring at my shoes?"

"The hairdresser . . ." I began, but she broke in, pointing to my pole. "Are you going fishing? If so, the aquarium is over there."

I remained rooted to the spot. She stared past me into the garden. "Oh, that awful gray," she said, "always gray. I was hoping a young man like you would bring a little color into my life. We have no children, my husband and I. How could we have? He doesn't look at me, doesn't touch me, doesn't even talk to me unless I squeeze the words out of him. And even then, he always speaks of himself in the third person and treats me as if I weren't there. At first I thought he was a shoe fetishist, but even when I'm not wearing shoes, he stares at my feet. Sometimes, when I ask him to look at me, he does at least raise his eyes and look at my knees. When you've refilled my glass again, I'll let you in on a secret."

I poured her some more wine. She leaned toward me and whispered, "I've lately had dreams in which I consist of nothing but feet and legs."

Startled, I raised my head and looked her in the face. "I assure you, madam . . ."

"Ah! An *I*! You're an *I*. I knew it: I can put myself in your hands. Anyone who produces such creations is capable of great things." She sprang to her feet. "I want you to create a hairstyle for me that will encourage him to look at me at last. Do you have your tussocks with you?" She looked around the room. "Never mind, I know just the one I want. It was on the table in the center of the arena."

I knew the one she meant. "Of course," I replied. "It'll suit you wonderfully well."

"Come on, then, let's not waste any more time." She hurried to a dressing table at the far end of the huge room and sat down at it. "Help yourself to a glass too," she called. "Better bring the decanter with you."

I did so, and a few moments later I was finger-deep in her dark, abundant hair. I removed the pins, let the hair fall to her shoulders, and picked up my scissors and comb, oblivious of time and space. After all my years of cutting men's hair, I was confronted by opportunities that made my heart race. My hands flew, seemingly in several places at once. Sometimes I was beside her, sometimes above her, sometimes kneeling at her feet, my scissors clattering like the beaks of a whole flock of storks. My creation gradually emerged until finally—finally—it became visible in its entirety. It was a daring structure composed of entwined lianas, an allegory of the aberrations and tribulations of life brought to a grandiose conclusion by the hand of a brilliant creator. Exhausted, I collapsed into a chair and closed my eyes for a moment.

When I opened them, Frau zu Bärenbaum was standing over me. "You didn't disappoint me," she said in a husky voice. "Now he'll look at me, now all will be well . . ."

# 10
## *Tonight we'll slaughter the swine!*

My assumption that the pocket-picking affair was settled proved to be premature. One of the men who had been relieved of his wallet seemed to harbor certain suspicions. "I can't rid myself of the feeling," he told me one afternoon, as I lay in a deck chair while *Liberty* neared the Canary Islands in glorious weather, "that I felt a hand touch my bottom that night. I felt sure I was mistaken and thought no more about it, but soon afterward, I noticed my wallet was missing, so it must have been a hand after all. What do you think?" He was standing over my deck chair as he spoke, his bulky figure blotting out the sun.

I looked up at him. "Your bottom, you say?"

"My bottom. My hip pocket, which is where I keep my wallet."

"There was a whole crowd standing around the table. Perhaps someone steadied himself against you when the ship rolled."

"Perhaps. But why did the wallet disappear?"

"Who was standing behind you?"

"From the feel of the hand, it must have been a lady."

I gestured to the vacant deck chair beside mine. "Sit down, and we'll order a drink. Skrik's my name."

"I know who you are, naturally—everyone on board does. You're the man who does the ladies' hair. An enviable profession." With a grunt, he lowered himself onto the deck chair. "My name is Baumhauer. I'm an employment agent."

"Who are you employing at present?"

He sighed. "A can of worms."

I remained silent, as I always did when I guessed that someone wanted to tell me something but didn't know how to begin.

After a while, Baumhauer laid a hand on my arm. "Tablecloths," he said. "A textile manufacturer in New Jersey who makes tablecloths. But not just any old tablecloths—works of art, you've never seen their like! I recruited some lacemakers for him in Bruges, the best! Twenty women. Now I'm escorting them across the Atlantic to New Jersey."

He said he had supplied the railroad industry with Russian track layers, the capitol in Washington with Italian plasterers, the bridges over the Hudson with German engineers, and the nouveaux riches of Newport with English gardeners, and he'd never had a problem—but now, in the case of these Belgian females, he was at his wits' end.

I still said nothing, and his fingers tightened on my arm.

"You're the expert on women. Help me and I'll forget about the wallet incident, which I suspect you witnessed." The problem I was to help him solve was this: the lacemakers were tired of traveling in second class.

I looked up at the flying jib, which had just filled with a *plop* as a gust of wind hit the ship. "Let's go inside, it's becoming chilly out here," I said, getting to my feet.

He gripped my arm again. "And you'll help me?"

"Yes, I'll have a word with them."

"All of them?"

"No, just the one who's making the biggest fuss. Send her to see me."

She strode into my cabin an hour later. I discovered I knew her. She was the most striking-looking young woman on board, a beautiful creature whose hair I had done two or three times for dinner. I stopped short—how had a second-class passenger come to be dining in the saloon?

She planted herself in front of me. "He's a swine!" she hissed.

"Who is?"

"Baumhauer. The man's a swine."

I said nothing.

In Bruges last winter, she told me, that swine had placed advertisements in the newspapers to the effect that an American firm would pay three dollars a day. Only the finest lacemakers would be considered. He held interviews at a hotel. Unemployed now that the European market had been swamped by lace from the British colonies, many young women from Bruges had applied, herself included. Their parents knew nothing about it and would never have agreed, except that swine had promised them first-class passage and lodgings *en famille* in the most respectable houses in New Jersey. He showed them letters from women he had already placed, and all were most enthusiastic.

They had to pay their own fares to Hamburg, but that swine promised to reimburse them upon their arrival in America. Then, when they embarked, it turned out that first class was fully booked. A clerical error, he told them—cabins would be vacated for them, but they would unfortunately have to sleep on the lower deck for the first few days. "You're familiar with the lower deck?"

I nodded, and her expression suggested that I had just confessed to cannibalism.

That swine had then taken to escorting them to dinner at the captain's table in the saloon—not all of them at once, of course, but one at a time, and he'd first had their hair done at his expense. "You remember me?"

I nodded again, and she looked at me as if my favorite fare were little children.

Over dinner, that swine had told her that the textile factory in New Jersey was seeking forewomen as well as lacemakers—at five dollars a day. Very few of them could be considered—probably only herself, in fact. He would be glad to discuss the matter in greater detail in his cabin after dinner, but it would be better if the others didn't know. "The discussion lasted until the next morning!" she said angrily.

The others had obviously found out after all. "What does he want you to do?" she demanded. "Why did he want me to speak with you? Why did he send me here?"

"I think he's afraid."

"Of me?"

"Of all of you."

"Then we mustn't disappoint him. Tonight—tonight we'll slaughter that swine. He's pocketed the first-class fares, and we're living in that hellhole down below!" She turned to go. "We'll come here an hour from now, so you can make us look nice for dinner."

"All of you?"

She nodded grimly.

"But they won't let you up top."

"We'll see about that . . ."

The commotion an hour later was considerable. At first some seamen were sent to bar the women's way. Then the galley hands were mobilized and, when even that proved insufficient, the captain ordered his first officer and Odysseus Hirsch to block the companionway up which the women were fighting their way step by step. "Swine! Swine! Swine!" they chanted as they thrust aside one man after another. It would have been easy enough for the seamen—all sturdy fellows—to stop the women, but the element of surprise, coupled with the women's fierce determination (not to mention the din they were making), operated in their favor. The men gave way and let them pass.

Baumhauer came storming into my cabin. "What have you done, you dunderhead! You must calm them down. What's this all about?"

"I couldn't do a thing. They simply said they'd slaughter you tonight."

He stared at me, his lips mutely shaping the word *slaughter*. Then he pleaded, "You must hide me!"

I was about to push him into my clothes closet when the first of the lacemakers rounded the corner. "Swine! Swine! Swine!" Seizing Baumhauer's arm, which was protruding from the closet, they dragged him out. Moments later, he was lying on the floor with the women bending over him, prodding him with their long wooden lacemakers' needles.

Surprisingly agile for a man of his bulk, Baumhauer rolled across the floor, lashing out in all directions and squirming this way and that. By this time, spectators were crowding around my cabin door. Odysseus Hirsch stationed himself in the doorway with outspread arms to prevent them from coming in. "There's nothing to see here!" he called. "Everything's fine. Please return to your cabins."

They didn't, of course.

Instead, the captain appeared. He was wearing his white full-dress uniform, complete with pith helmet, and holding a baton in his hand. He looked like royalty, and silence fell when he entered. "Ladies," he said solemnly. "At this moment, we are thousands of fathoms above the ocean floor. The same distance upward would take us almost to heaven. We are floating, as it were, between the highest heights and the deepest depths imaginable, the same heights and depths that separate the human soul from heaven and hell. I come from a family that never saw the sea. My ancestors knew nothing but their plowed fields and the sunshine and rain that enabled their crops to ripen, yet they allowed me my dreams, even as a child. When I sat in the puddle behind the pigsty and saw the sky reflected in it, I came to believe that there is no difference between above and below, rich and poor, good and bad. In later years, the sea matured that idea into a certainty. We are afloat in a nutshell and always see the same thing, regardless of whether we look up or down. Humility, ladies—humility is what the sea has taught me, not despair. It is humility that enables us to conquer despair and transform it into hope. I have probably passed over this spot in the ocean a hundred times. I cannot claim to know every fish making its way along far below us, or every star that twinkles in the sky above us, but I can sense them—sense them, filled with humility and profound emotion. How often have I believed that the end was near when, in a severe storm, we bailed masses of water back into the sea with our bare hands, when we grieved for men who had gone overboard, or when our supplies were running out? That is when people need people, souls that are close to them, hearts that beat in unison with their own. At such moments, the sea tells us that we may survive, that it is granting us a deferment—that the drowning comrade is only anticipating what awaits us all in time. And if we risk our own lives in trying to save him after all, it is that certainty that inspires us and lends us the strength to perform superhuman feats.

"Ladies, this is your first experience of the sea. Believe me, you will not be the same hereafter. Perhaps one or another of you can already sense what it is doing to you: transforming you into people who can forgive and forget, who are developing the magnanimity that enables you to sense that the sky above us and the seabed beneath us are one and the same. The little boy in his puddle behind the pigsty was granted that insight, and I wish with all my heart and soul that you, dear ladies, will be granted it too. I should consider it an honor if you would now accompany me to my private saloon to seal that wish with the aid of a decent drop to drink."

He looked at the lacemakers one by one, his little eyes above their enormous pouches as deep as the ocean. "If you would follow me," he said, turning to go. He paused briefly beside the employment agent, who was still sprawled on the floor, and told Odysseus Hirsch, "Clap him in irons."

Baumhauer was not clapped in irons, of course, just escorted to his cabin soon afterward, but the lacemakers enjoyed an unforgettable evening in the captain's private saloon. Before long, they could be heard laughing and drumming on the table with their needles while the captain sang them sea shanties. The rum seemed to have quickly dispelled their anger and made them forget about their plan to slaughter "that swine." The captain evidently enjoyed their company too, because he invited them to his saloon every evening after dinner for the rest of the voyage. He could not, of course, offer them any first-class cabins, because these were all taken—but they seemed unworried by this as they made their way back to their bunks in the bowels of the ship. The hour was late, but they came back singing.

# 11

# *I've wrestled with bullocks and lifted sea lions*

The cabin next to my hairdressing salon was occupied by the ship's doctor, Heimo Servatius, who used it as his workplace, just as I did mine. It was the *Liberty*'s medical center. Our proximity proved practical, because most of his patients used his products to embellish their appearance. A round-shouldered but agile little man, Servatius owned patents on a number of tinctures he had developed for tightening skin, as well as powders beneficial to the waistline because of their laxative effect. He also purveyed head packs of the fuller's earth he kept in casks, which were said to promote hair growth if applied regularly. For female patients who had just consulted him, what could be more natural than to sit down in my salon and have the earth washed out of their hair?

He seldom treated the sick, most of whom came on stormy days when seasickness was rife. On this voyage, however, he was very busy ministering to a chronic invalid, a woman who had initially come to his medical center but whom he now treated in her cabin. Pernille

Jakobsson by name, she hailed from Denmark, where she had been a star performer at the Tivoli Gardens in Copenhagen, and was now on her way to America to take up an engagement with the Ringling Bros. Circus. However, her prospects of being able to continue her career in the New World were not good, Servatius confided to me, because she was suffering from an occlusion of the gullet that rendered her incapable of swallowing a morsel without instantly gagging. He had initially thought that she was suffering from a particularly stubborn form of seasickness, but her condition had since become chronic. She was rapidly losing weight, which could not have been worse—because Pernille Jakobsson, who had scored great success as a wrestler at the Tivoli, was scheduled to appear with Ringling Bros. Circus as "The Strongest Woman in the World." There could be no question of this at present, said Servatius. "She's steadily losing weight," he told me in a tone of genuine regret. "She's just a shadow of her former self. Every time she sees herself in the mirror, she bursts into tears." What he wanted me to do was call on her in her cabin and do her hair. He had developed a theory that patients should be treated not only from the inside out, but from the outside in: if Pernille Jakobsson could look at herself in the mirror again and feel satisfied with her appearance, it might dispel her internal resistance to the ingestion of food.

At first I could see no sign of Pernille Jakobsson when I went in. The cabin was full of costumes and sportswear, the floor strewn with dumbbells, weights, and chest expanders, the bulkhead plastered with newspaper clippings devoted to her exploits. Silver laurel wreaths were lying around, together with certificates and cups. There was a blanket draped over a chair, and it was not until something stirred beneath it that I became aware of Pernille's presence. Only her head was visible, but it captured my attention. Her long, flaxen hair was gathered into a braid that swung to and fro in time to the movements of the ship. The hair was matted and lifeless, but I could tell that it had once been magnificent.

I cleared another chair and sat down facing her. The blanket rose and fell with her breathing, which rattled a little, but that was the only sound she made. Silence reigned for a while. Lying at my feet was an iron bar with weights attached to the ends. I kicked it, but it didn't budge an inch. I bent down and gripped the bar, but it wasn't until I enlisted the help of my other hand that I managed to lift it a little way off the floor. I was about to put it down when a hand emerged from the blanket. With difficulty, I raised it high enough for the hand to grasp it, whereupon the dumbbell rose and fell at a rate of knots, again and again, as if it were light as a French loaf. It was then handed back to me, and I replaced it on the floor.

What on earth was this woman capable of when in full possession of her strength? I picked up one of the silver cups and examined it. Not knowing Danish, I couldn't read the inscription.

"Skagen 1873, champion at all weights," she said. She had lowered the blanket a few inches and was staring at the cup. "Shoulder throw, 210 kilograms."

"The weight of your female opponent, you mean?"

"My female opponent? It was a young bull."

"You've wrestled with bulls?"

"I've lifted sea lions too."

I rose and stood behind her. "Your hair—I'd like to undo it."

She didn't reply. I carefully proceeded to undo her braid.

"I've pulled hay wagons with that," she remarked. "You want to cut it off?"

"Not on your life! Were the wagons loaded?"

"Not always. You're a hairdresser?"

"Yes. Dr. Servatius sent me. He thinks I could do you some good."

"You're doing that already. What comes next?"

"I'd like to oil your hair and massage your scalp."

She removed the blanket from her face completely. Her cheeks were sunken and her lips limp, but her throat and neck were muscular and sinewy.

"How old am I? Guess!"

"I never guess women's ages. I respect them far too much."

Her arm shot out, and her fingers gripped my wrist like a vise. "How old?"

"Half as old as I am, plus six years."

She nodded and let me go, then pulled the blanket back over her face and put her head back.

Having undone her braid, I massaged the oil into her hair, starting at the hairline and ending at the tips.

"I even wrestled in the womb—with myself. Or so my mother said, anyway."

"Was she a wrestler too?"

No, said Pernille, her mother had been a pastor—the first woman in Denmark to ascend a pulpit. She was small and dainty, almost invisible beneath her cassock. But her voice! When she called Pernille to meals, she was audible in the next village, and when she concluded her sermons by describing the torments of hell and enjoining the congregation to virtue and propriety, some of the worshipers put their fingers in their ears. Others wept.

Glistening with oil, Pernille's hair now hung down almost to the floor. I began to massage her scalp.

Her mother had been born with this mighty voice, she went on. Her first cry had scared the midwife so much, she dispensed with payment for her services provided she could leave the house as quickly as possible. The women of the family had all been endowed with special attributes. Her mother's mother, for example, could recall every sentence she had ever heard in her life, and *her* mother could bring water to a boil with her bare hands, simply by immersing them in it. Pernille herself had overcome everything in her path, even as a little girl. Her future as a wrestler had been clearly mapped out from the start.

I wrapped her hair in a towel and wound it around her head. Tomorrow I would wash the oil out, I told her, but it must be left to sink in until then. Then I asked her if she would exercise once more, just for me. She extended both arms from the woolen blanket and, with a considerable effort, I placed a dumbbell in each hand. She was still pumping them up and down when I left the cabin a few minutes later.

The following day, I found Pernille in the same position I had left her in the previous evening. I couldn't tell if she had even risen from the chair, although there were indications that someone had visited her in the meantime: some fruit had been left on the table in an evident attempt to stimulate her appetite.

Having decided to do her hair another good turn, I had come equipped with some of Dr. Servatius's fuller's earth. I began by undoing the towel, which was wound around Pernille's head like a turban. Then I placed a bowl on the floor and rinsed her hair with a watering can. I had to rinse it several times before the last of the oil had been washed out, after which I worked the earth into her hair.

That smell, said Pernille from under her blanket—that smell reminded her of the happiest days of her childhood, when the summer rain seemed never-ending and the ground was so soft, no cart could cross it for fear of getting stuck in the mud. That was when she liked to camp out on the edge of the woods, where the scent of earth was particularly strong, and burrow into the warm, moist soil. She felt herself absorb its strength, and in her dreams she became one of the roots that supplied the trees with nourishment.

She extended a finger from under the blanket. "Would you let me have a taste?"

I put some fuller's earth on her fingertip. The finger withdrew, and I heard her suck it.

"Were you already hauling carts by your hair at that time?" I asked.

"No, not yet," Pernille replied, extending her finger again. "Do you know why I was so fond of trees? They were a match for me." No one else was a match for her by the time she reached puberty, she said—only trees refused to be beaten. She went into the woods again and again and tried to wrestle one to the ground, but she couldn't.

I washed the earth out of her hair and told her I would dress it the next day. When I was about to leave, she put out her hands for the dumbbells, which I gave her. The jar of earth, which was still half full, I left behind.

I had difficulty concealing my surprise when she entered my hairdressing salon the next afternoon. She was holding the empty jar and wearing a red costume embroidered with silver sequins. It covered only her trunk and left her arms and legs bare. Dr. Servatius had not been exaggerating: Pernille Jakobsson was thin, almost bony, and the costume that had presumably been skintight was all puckered.

It was a traveling circus that had extricated her from the parental parsonage at the age of fourteen, she told me as she sat there while I inserted curlers, having decided to set her wonderful flaxen hair in as many ringlets as possible. She enjoyed going to the circus, like all children, but had never imagined it would someday be her world. That year, though, she did not leave the circus tent when the afternoon performance was over. A man named Hercules had prompted that decision.

Accompanied by a roll on the drums, Hercules had appeared from behind a curtain wearing a costume like the one she was wearing now. He strode around the ring several times, glaring wildly at the audience as if looking for someone. And then he found her: Lydia, chained to a stake with a bull snorting and pawing the sand in front of her. Hercules flung out his arms, called her name, and promised to release her. First, however, he had to overcome numerous obstacles: he wrestled with a giant who barred his path, flooring him after applying a few holds; a snake coiled itself around his body, but he flung it out of the ring; a polar bear pounced on him, but he hoisted it into the air and put it to flight. He then confronted the bull, which he gripped by the horns and wrestled to the ground. Finally, when he had released Lydia from her chains, a pony came trotting up, and the pair rode out of the circus tent to thunderous applause.

After the performance, Pernille sat alone in the arena until Lydia came to tell her that Hercules was expecting her.

Pernille was ever so slightly disappointed to learn that his real name was Hendrik Larsson, and that he was the son of the ringmaster. Not only did he also sell tickets at the entrance, but he also dressed up as a clown and splashed front-row spectators with water, swung from the big top as a trapeze artiste, sold soft drinks during intermission, and made ponies dance waltzes on their hind legs. Lydia's name really was Lydia. She was his second wife and his partner in the knife-throwing act.

Hercules—he permitted Pernille to go on calling him that—compensated his young fan amply for her disappointment by entrusting the circus animals to her care. She became so fond of the bull and the polar bear, both of which were extremely docile and affectionate, that she couldn't help shedding a tear, even today, whenever she thought of them. She had spent four years traveling the length and breadth of Denmark with the circus. Pitching and striking the big top, transporting the cages, cleaning the trailers—she loved all her jobs, but it never occurred to her to enter the ring herself.

One day, however, the time came. Hercules slipped on a puddle during his clown act and sprained his ankle. He completed his act limping badly—the spectators found that particularly funny—but sat outside the tent while the ring was being prepared for Lydia's rescue with his foot in a bowl of cold water and his face contorted with pain. His ankle was steadily swelling from minute to minute.

Pernille reacted swiftly and without thinking. Having donned her red leotard, she entered the ring the moment the drumroll began. The giant screamed in agony as she threw him to the ground, the polar bear fled from her, and she snapped off one of the poor bull's horns in the process of subduing it. Her greatest challenge, however, was Lydia: she resisted fiercely when Pernille tried to release her, called repeatedly for her husband, and demanded to be left alone. Pernille had no choice but to carry her bodily out of the ring, complete with the stake to which she was chained.

The audience went wild, but that wasn't all: after the performance—Hercules and Lydia had shut themselves up in their trailer and told Pernille to get lost—she was accosted by a man who offered her a contract as a wrestler at the Tivoli Gardens.

Might I prevail on her to spend the night sitting up, I asked her, because her hair must dry out completely before I removed the curlers, and that would take until tomorrow.

She had been accustomed to sitting up throughout the voyage, she said, and had never used her bunk so far. Then she asked if I could help her to obtain a little more fuller's earth. Dr. Servatius's proximity proved practical once again, and when Pernille Jakobsson left my salon soon afterward, she was carrying a fresh jar under her arm.

After I had spruced up my last customer of the day in preparation for her dinner at the captain's table and cleaned my equipment, someone tapped on the open door of my cabin and asked if he might come in. It was the pianist whom I had often seen playing for passengers in the saloon at night. He was already dressed for dinner in an immaculately fitting tailcoat and coarse woolen mittens. "I'm Vladimir Gospodin," he said. "You were kind enough to show me to my cabin on the day we sailed."

I remembered him well. He had been carrying a small, shabby briefcase in the crook of his arm, clasping it to him as if it might escape.

Of course I remembered him, I said. We were honored to have such a famous pianist on board.

"Who is the lady who was with you this afternoon?" he blurted out. "The lady in the red leotard?" He had apparently seen her entering my salon.

I must have looked a trifle disparaging, because he hastened to add that his intentions were only the best. He thought he had recognized her, he said, and if she was the person he thought she was, she was a heroine—no, more than that, a shining light!

"We hairdressers are reputed to be gossips," I rejoined, "and certainly not without reason. Some of my colleagues promptly pass on all they've just heard from one customer to another. If the customer has said nothing, they recount things they've made up themselves."

He waved the mittens he doubtless wore to protect his sensitive fingers. No, no, he said, he would never impute anything of the kind to me. Might he sit down?

He wore his long, wavy hair loose in the style familiar from busts of Beethoven or Schubert. It was becoming thin enough on top for his scalp to show through, so I took comb and scissors and backcombed it to hide his bald spot. He hailed from Moscow, he told me. His father and mother had both been pianists, likewise his grandparents and his brothers and sisters. The one exception was his twin brother, Oleg, who lived in San Francisco and had panned enough gold in California to make him moderately wealthy. Six months earlier, Vladimir had received a letter from Oleg begging him to come to America. He was in possession of a map on which some immensely productive veins of gold were marked, and enclosed in the letter was a copy of the map that he had made.

"Do you still have the map?" I asked.

Of course, he said. It was in his briefcase, from which he was never parted except when going to dinner. If I was interested, he would gladly show it to me tomorrow.

He hadn't hesitated to comply with Oleg's request. The years of separation from his brother had been terrible, he said—ordinary people had no idea how close a bond existed between twins. Oleg had never stirred from his side when he toured Europe as a pianist: he had sat beside Vladimir in concert halls and turned the pages, had carried his luggage and negotiated his contracts with impresarios. The thought of not spending every minute of the day with Oleg had been farther from his mind than any galaxy—until the incident at the Tivoli. That had changed everything.

Copenhagen was one of his favorite concert venues—the acoustics of its Konzerthaus were second to none. It was not for nothing that Brahms and Liszt had scored their greatest successes there, and he could, in all modesty, say that the same applied to himself. His recitals had sold out on three successive nights, bouquets by the dozen had landed on the stage, and women had forced their way into his dressing room and made advances that still caused him to blush with embarrassment.

And indeed, the bald spot on his head turned red as he was telling me this.

Then his brother had told him about this offer from the Tivoli. It seemed that in the Underwater World, a huge aquarium in which exotic fish were kept, a school of Australian stingrays had mystified balletomanes and biologists by performing synchronized evolutions to a certain piano sonata by Albinoni. However, the fish would do this only if the sonata were played double-time, a feat of which very few pianists were capable. One of those, said Vladimir Gospodin, was himself.

The night the musical experiment took place, dozens of scientists from various disciplines gathered at the Tivoli's invitation. The aquarium, a rotunda several yards in diameter, had rows of chairs arranged around it and a piano positioned in front of it. The lights were extinguished until only the aquarium and, of course, the piano keyboard were illuminated.

Although predicted, what happened was nonetheless incredible: after the first few bars of the sonata, the stingrays detached themselves from the other circling fish and gathered together in front of the piano. When the stately introduction was followed by an excitingly rhythmical allegro, its effect reinforced by being played double-time, the rays began to dance. They turned in a circle, spread out and converged, rotated on the spot, swam synchronously left and right, halted abruptly, and fluttered their long stingers. The scientists rose from their chairs and crowded forward, transfixed by the spectacle before their eyes. They stared so intently at the rays' formation dance, they failed at first to notice that the walls of the aquarium were fracturing. It was not until a vertical crack appeared and quickly snaked in both directions, like the branches of a tree, that the first cries of alarm rang out. Then the glass wall burst asunder, and water came surging out into the auditorium.

While recounting this, Vladimir Gospodin gazed at the mirror as if he could see the fish dancing in front of him. When he got to the part where the aquarium disintegrated, he jumped up, staring at me wildly, and tottered out of the cabin with the comb still embedded in his backcombed hair.

When Pernille Jakobsson visited me the next morning to have the curlers removed, she was wearing a white costume with a broad silver belt encircling her waist. Her pale face had acquired a little color, and her cheeks no longer looked quite as sunken. Noticing my appraising gaze, she paused in front of me and turned on the spot so I could admire her from every angle. "This is how I used to appear," she said. "I was the White Amazon, one of the Tivoli's main attractions."

But not right away, of course. The agent who had recruited her for the Tivoli introduced her to her new role by degrees. First he made her appear in the lady wrestlers' tent, where she fought in a big tub of mud with women who, though big and extremely heavy, were weak by Pernille's standards. Within a few weeks, none of them would fight her, so it was suggested that she wrestle with men. She didn't object to this in principle, but she wasn't prepared to pretend to be a man. The Tivoli management had problems with this, but the temptation was too great; Pernille was already pulling in the crowds.

When the first poster went up in town advertising a match between the White Amazon and a male wrestler known as the Aarhus Bull, all hell broke loose. Women's associations marched through the streets of Copenhagen in protest, church representatives invoked Christian values, and a delegation from city hall appeared at the Tivoli and announced that the event had been banned. But it was already too late for that: on the day of the match, thousands of rubbernecks appeared outside the gates, and when they eventually opened, there were more people outside the tent than could find seats inside it.

The match lasted only a few seconds. The opponent's agent had tried in vain to talk Pernille into agreeing on the length of the bout in advance and had promised her money, but the Aarhus Bull didn't stand a chance. After flying out of the ring twice in quick succession, he did not return. This did not improve the situation: the spectators, who wanted their money's worth, crowded ever closer to the ring, and some of them climbed over the ropes to avoid being crushed. Pernille hurled them out one by one, to the accompaniment of delighted yells from the onlookers.

Her hair was now a halo made up of countless golden ringlets. I was satisfied with my work and eagerly awaited her reaction, but she merely glanced at herself in the mirror, nodded curtly, and went on talking. Her agent had informed her the next day that he could find no more opponents for her, and that they must think of something else. That was how she found her true vocation: fighting wild animals.

No, she said, she had always done her best not to hurt them seriously. The Tivoli established a zoo that soon became extremely popular with the inhabitants of Copenhagen, and it was from this that she selected her opponents. Buffalo, bears, orangutans, wild boar—she beat them all, sometimes more than one at a time. Only one kind of animal was safe from her, and that was the shark, for Pernille could not swim.

Several of those wonderful creatures were kept in the Tivoli's new aquarium, which was the biggest in the world, and she would often sit there watching the elegant swimmers. Her face-to-face encounter with them, which was entirely unforeseen, occurred when she witnessed that incredible experiment with the dancing stingrays, which presented a choreographic performance to piano accompaniment.

She was standing a little apart from the audience, so she didn't at first grasp why panic had broken out. Then, when people started running past her, she saw five sharks come gliding into the auditorium with the escaping flood. The pianist was so engrossed in his playing, he failed to see the creatures bearing down on him and snapping at his legs. Pernille dashed forward, seized the fish one after another, and hurled them aside. One of them closed its teeth on her braid and tugged at it, whereupon she whirled it around her head and flung it to the other end of the auditorium by centrifugal force. She lost part of her braid in the process, unfortunately, but—as I could see, she said—it had grown back.

Pernille looked around and asked if there was any fuller's earth left. I brought her a jar from Dr. Servatius's stock, after which she rose, thanked me for the successful hairdo, and departed.

The following evening, Dr. Servatius came dashing into my cabin, seized my arm, and towed me outside. I mustn't miss this, he kept exclaiming. I must see this! A resurrection had occurred: Pernille Jakobsson had appeared for dinner. Through the door of the saloon, we saw the passengers seated at their tables, with the lady wrestler in the place of honor beside the captain. A few tables away sat Vladimir Gospodin, staring at Pernille wide-eyed. When everyone was seated, he rose and applauded her. More and more passengers joined in without really knowing why. Eventually, Pernille stood up and thanked them with a gracious smile. When the applause died away and people addressed themselves to their soup, she and the pianist continued to stand there, gazing at each other across the tables.

Late that night, when the lacemakers had retired to their quarters from the captain's cabin, singing happily, faint piano music could be heard coming from the saloon. Peering around the door, I saw Pernille Jakobsson standing behind Vladimir Gospodin, who was seated at the piano with his eyes shut, playing the Albinoni sonata for her. The lady wrestler, whose hands were resting on his shoulders, was swaying almost imperceptibly in time to the music.

# 12
# *Diabolical bellowing*

I first noticed the bottle when I knocked it over with my foot. It was standing outside my door—someone must have left it there during the night—and it rolled into my cabin because the *Liberty* was contending with rough seas and groaning as she heeled from side to side. A wine bottle without a label or any form of inscription that might have supplied information about its source, it was corked and unopened and evidently contained red wine.

My first thought was of Serge, the ship's cook. My old Ukrainian friend sometimes gave me little presents in the shape of particularly tasty dishes or special drinks, usually when he wanted something from me.

On our last voyage, for example, he had requested my help when a passenger complained of having found several hairs in her asparagus soup—a whole tuft of them, in fact. She had fished it out and marched indignantly across the saloon, waving the tuft like a trophy. Serge was summoned to see the captain, who gave him notice in the lady's presence. This had often helped to placate passengers who found something not to their satisfaction. The lady was assured that she would not have to undergo such an experience the next time she sailed on the *Liberty*, and that appeased her.

But in this case, Serge refused to be beaten. He was unaware of being at fault, and although he would of course be aboard on the next voyage and all future voyages because he was the captain's brother-in-law—and it didn't matter to the passengers anyway, because they were unlikely to emigrate again aboard the *Liberty*—he wouldn't let the matter rest. He visited me in my cabin, bringing an excellent sorbet, and told me for the umpteenth time about his wife, who had left him because she thought it insufficient to see him only once a year. She did give birth to one child per annum, but that was really the most he could do for her, he said, because he was a ship's cook, and Irina had known that from the first. Touched as ever, I assured him that he could count on my friendship at all times, and what could I do for him on this occasion?

It was about the tuft of hair, he said. He was sure it hadn't been floating in the bowl when the soup was served. I had done the lady's hair several times. Had I noticed anything relevant? Having brought the tuft with him, Serge handed it to me. I recognized its provenance at once, of course. While I was massaging her head, the lady in question had confided to me that hair loss was her biggest problem—far more serious than the fact that her husband, a former artillery officer, was dishonorably discharged from the army because his habit of marching in waltz time had thrown whole companies into disarray; far more serious still than his shouting "Fire!" when making love to her and imitating the sound of a cannonball landing in the midst of a field kitchen.

I promised Serge that I would see to the matter.

When the lady came to me for her last appointment before we reached New York, I told her, "Now, let's see if we can help you leave this ship looking a million dollars." And I backcombed her sparse hair like mad. She watched in the mirror, wide-eyed, as I created a hairdo as thick and firm as any hairdo could be. Last of all, I took the tuft Serge had given me and wove it artistically into the summit of her towering coiffure.

Where had I found her missing hairpiece? she demanded. On learning the truth, she was beside herself with dismay. That poor man, she exclaimed, what had she done to him? She had never felt so ashamed in her life. That evening, she went to the captain and implored him to revoke the cook's dismissal. When, after much hesitation, he agreed, she fervently embraced him and everyone else she met on the way back to her cabin.

She really did look a million dollars when she descended the gangway in New York. I was standing at the rail with Odysseus Hirsch as she turned for a moment and blew me a kiss.

So it was Serge—the wine must have come from him. A little while later, I walked into the galley with the bottle in my hand. To my surprise, Serge assured me he'd never seen it before, nor did he have any favor to ask of me. He did, however, suggest that we open the bottle and sample its contents. After the first mouthful, he solemnly sat down on a stool and stared at his glass. French, Bordeaux, marlaceous soil, probably southwest-facing, a very old vintage that harbored all the secrets of the vine. He couldn't remember when he had last tasted so magnificent a wine, and he asked me where the bottle had come from.

When I told him I had assumed until a minute ago that he was the anonymous donor, he slowly shook his head. For this bottle, he said, I would have owed him a quid pro quo I could never have paid and he would never have asked of me; a wine of this quality was worth at least one murder, if not more. He offered to store the bottle correctly until we could find a worthy occasion on which to finish it.

The next morning, I found another bottle outside my cabin and, standing a few feet away, two gentlemen who said, *"Bonjour, monsieur."*

They spoke as simultaneously as they bowed and extended their hands. Clearly twins, they were short, thickset men of around forty, both wearing Basque berets.

"We hope we didn't startle you," one of them said in French-accented German. "Permit me to address you, as my brother does not speak your language." They shook hands with me simultaneously, this being possible only because the brother who spoke no German was left-handed. "My brother is left-handed," the speaker confirmed. Their names were Claude and Camillo Dagorne, he told me. They were on their way from their native Bordeaux to California, and they had a problem. They wondered if I could spare them a few minutes of my doubtless invaluable time, if possible right away. They bowed in unison and awaited my answer in that position. Since I was not expecting my first customer until eleven o'clock, I was able to oblige. Camillo asked me to follow them.

We went down into the bowels of the *Liberty*, made our way past the stable and the second-class accommodations to the stern, then descended another companionway. When the Frenchmen paused outside the sternmost door, water could be heard sloshing around in the bilges beneath us. Behind this door lay the storeroom containing passengers' possessions not wanted on the voyage. They led me along the row of lockers and came to a halt in front of one of them. It was empty, save for three wooden crates.

Camillo lit a kerosene lamp and handed it to me. Inside the crates were some small, gnarled plants with drooping, withered leaves. They could not stand the salty air, Camillo explained. It was a disaster. These crates contained his and his brother's entire fortune, their future, their livelihood. From Bordeaux's finest marlaceous soil, southwest-facing, ancient vines that harbored all the secrets of the wine they produced, plants for which many people would do anything, even commit murder. And now this!

I asked if I might touch the vines. Of course, said Camillo, they yearned for the touch of a hand—they missed the sun, the air, and, above all, human attention. He and his brother came down here every day because the vines were not allowed on deck for reasons of plant hygiene—they had been allowed to bring them aboard on that condition alone—but their visits were not enough.

Putting down the bottle, which I was still carrying, I stroked the withered leaves. "Serge says your wine is the best he ever tasted," I told them.

"It *is* the best, and once we plant our vineyards in California, the whole world will know it! But who knows if that will ever happen? You can see for yourself . . ."

I crouched down and carefully massaged one leaf after another. The brothers sat down beside me. There had once been a similarly dramatic situation, said Camillo. At that time, the vineyard near Bordeaux had still belonged to his grandfather, Charles Dagorne, who had also been mayor, postmaster, and captain of the local boules team. Boules was a serious business in those days, not a Sunday morning pastime for old men while the women prepared lunch at home—no, boules was a point of honor. One did not refer to years numerically; they were known as "The Year We Beat Saint-Georges" or "The Year We Won the Championship." Years in which no titles were won did not rate a mention. If someone unlucky enough to be born in such a year was asked the year of his birth, he replied, "A dead year."

In Charles Dagorne's day, there were no dead years—his team always won some title or other, and the Dagorne name still inspired respect in the area around Bordeaux. But he also aroused envy. Their grandfather had often received immoral propositions from other towns. He was offered substantial sums if he would help another team win a boules match by getting his team to lose, but he always refused as a matter of course. Then, however, someone hit upon the diabolical idea of sabotaging his vineyard.

One spring, when Charles Dagorne inspected his vines, which were just beginning to sprout, his blood ran cold: several of them had withered. Someone had sprinkled salt around the trunks. At first he thought it was frost, but then he realized that his vineyard was the victim of sabotage.

It did not take him long to work out who was behind this atrocity: it could only be the men from Saint-Georges, who were insufferable in any case. They were some of the worst losers at boules in the region. After one recent defeat, they had bombarded innocent goats with their boules, hitting one on the head and impairing its sense of balance so badly that it would have to spend the rest of its life lying down. Anyone capable of such a thing must also be guilty of this malicious raid.

The very next night, Grandfather Dagorne and his six best boules players stole into Saint-Georges and retaliated. Taking the town's stud bull from its stable—it had won more prizes than any other bull in the district, they grudgingly acknowledged—they led it into the local church. There they tied it up behind the chancel, pulled a sack over its head, and attached its tail to the bell ropes. By the time they left the town unobserved the way they had come, bells were ringing and diabolical bellowing was coming from the church.

Two nights later, more vines were salted; and the night after that, the verger of Saint-Georges awoke with a start to find hens cackling and pecking on his bed. After the next application of salt, the inhabitants of Saint-Georges found their schoolroom anointed with liquid manure from the dung heap.

Things might have gone on like this indefinitely, said Camillo, if all the owners of southwest-facing vineyards had not received a letter from the board of agriculture instructing them to drench their vines with sheep's milk to overcome the mildew that was currently rife and had already ravaged many a vineyard. By this time, three-quarters of Grandfather Dagorne's vines had died.

. . .

When I brought Serge the second bottle of wine, coupled with a request to store that one properly as well, and told him the story of the Dagornes, he at once knew what to do: the ship's lone sheep, he said—that sheep was a gift from God. Its milk might help us save the vines. If it had helped on one occasion, it might do so again. There would be no more fresh yogurt, admittedly, but it wasn't very popular with the passengers anyway. The animal had been earmarked for slaughter in the near future, but there couldn't be a better reason for sparing its life.

I accompanied Serge to the storeroom and held the ewe by its halter while he milked it. From now on, he proposed to milk the animal daily. This would be bound to increase milk production and benefit the vines, he said as he inspected the result: only a small bowlful the first day, but still, it was a start.

In order to enable each plant to benefit from the milk, he doled it out in dribs and drabs and rubbed it into the trunk just above the roots. They really were a pathetic sight, he lamented as he eyed the limp leaves before returning to his galley. I lingered a while longer, gently massaging the leaves twixt thumb and forefinger.

Grandfather had not lived to see the remnants of his vineyard saved, Camillo told me—he had died immediately after the catastrophe. His funeral was attended by delegations from every boules team in the *département*. Then five years old, Camillo and Claude would never forget the moment when each team captain stepped forward in turn and, as a token of respect, placed a boule in the coffin in which Charles Dagorne was lying in state. On the way to the churchyard, the pallbearers' legs buckled because of the coffin's immense weight, and a few yards before their destination, their strength gave out. The coffin hit the ground with a crash, the lid came off, and Grandfather and the boules rolled out and came to rest beside the open grave.

This incident estranged Dagorne's two sons, one of whom—Christian—was Claude and Camillo's father. He had been against inviting the rival boules teams to the funeral from the first, but what transformed the sons into mortal enemies was their struggle to inherit the vineyard. Charles Dagorne had stipulated in his will that the future owner of the vineyard would be whichever of his sons had the most children. For as long as this issue remained undecided, they would be equally responsible for producing the wine and share equally in the income it generated.

Claude and Camillo were the firstborn and, for the time being, only children of Christian Dagorne and his wife, Claudine, and their parents had really intended to leave it at that. Now, however, everything had changed. Their father and their uncle amended their family planning to accord with Grandfather's will, so every passing year produced an additional child. Neither of the brothers gained a lead, however—the match remained a draw, so they proceeded to beget children outside the family circle as well. Not only did this lead to fierce altercations with the legitimate husbands of the women involved, but the situation became utterly confused when they started to offer financial assistance to single mothers leading lonely, poverty-stricken lives because they had been expelled from their village communities, the said financial assistance being an inducement to name them as the fathers of their illegitimate children. Ten years after Charles Dagorne's death, both men claimed fifty-three children as their own, and the issue was still undecided.

The vineyard recovered and the wine brought record prices, so the sons and their families were in no financial difficulty. They could both have lived on it comfortably until they died, but they were eaten up with the desire to fulfill the terms of their father's will, each to his own advantage.

And then, one day, Christian Dagorne was found lying dead beside the track through the vineyard, crushed by an overturned donkey cart. Camillo never believed it was an accident, he said, not even when their uncle, who was now sole owner of the vineyard, assured the twins that he would regard them as his own children—that they had nothing to fear and would one day be sole heirs to the property, being the oldest children in the family. Fifteen at this time, they swore to avenge their father.

Our daily visits to the vines in the bowels of the *Liberty* did not go unnoticed. Betty was the first to wrinkle her nose while seated in my hairdressing chair. My hands smelled so fresh and tangy, she said—of soil and leaves, as if I'd just been working in a garden. I told her about our activities in the storeroom and added that I ought really to devote more time to the vines, which had suffered badly in the past and needed more attention than they were getting at present. Betty relieved me of my leaf massaging from then on, and I also enlisted Franziska von Hausendorf in our rescue attempts. She even volunteered to lend the vines the prison straw from her pillow, at least temporarily, and we laid it carefully around their trunks.

Happily, the ewe's milk yield had increased considerably, as Serge had foreseen. Rather than having to tote a pail of milk through the ship several times a day, he took the animal to the storeroom and milked it there. The vines were now the center of many comings and goings.

The Dagornes, who continued to prosper, once more found themselves the object of envy. Guards were posted to prevent vines from being stolen, Camillo recounted, and after some time little sentry boxes were installed around the vineyard and occupied by armed men. But vines continued to disappear. Uncle Alphonse suspected the guards themselves but could find no evidence against them, and he was seldom there in any case. After succeeding Grandfather as mayor, beautifying the town, and building a new school, a church, and an aqueduct for irrigating the fields, he rose to become prefect of the *département* and, eventually, a deputy in Bordeaux. The one office he refused to relinquish was the captaincy of the local boules team. It was this that ultimately led to the disaster that exempted Claude and Camillo from having to avenge their father's death in person.

The regional boules championship of 1874 was hosted, as usual, by the previous year's champions—in other words, by Dagorne, as the town had now been renamed. The last, decisive ball of the final match was reserved for the captain of the team, and it was Uncle Alphonse, of all people, who threw it far too short. The unimaginable had happened: Dagorne had lost. The town promptly erupted. Howling with rage and disappointment, the citizens of Dagorne spontaneously joined forces with the cheering victors from Saint-Georges, who had waited forty years for this day. Seizing pitchforks, shovels, and torches, they stormed the Dagornes' vineyard and made short work of it. Claude and Camillo, who had foreseen this disaster, got there just before them with a horse and cart, swiftly dug up as many vines as they could, and conveyed them to safety. The vineyard went up in flames soon afterward.

These were the only vines that had escaped the inferno, said Camillo, pointing to the crates. He and Claude had made it to Hamburg after a long and arduous journey, and here they were on board the *Liberty*. They intended to settle in California's Napa Valley, where the soil was the most marlaceous, resurrect their grandfather's vineyard, and found a town named Dagorne. Then the brothers invited Serge, Betty, Franziska, and me to their cabin to share a bottle of their miraculous wine.

# 13
## *These people can cook, I'll grant them that*

Lydia zu Bärenbaum's changed appearance had repercussions in the garrison town. Fifty-two officers' wives lived there, and they all knew each other—naturally, because there was nothing for them to do but meet for cards at each other's houses before getting themselves driven home in time to meet their husbands when they were off duty. During maneuvers or at other exceptional times, not even their husbands' company was available. Thus, even a minor deviation from the norm was welcome to them—and Lydia zu Bärenbaum's hairdo was a big deviation, bigger than I could ever have dreamed while creating it.

The first reaction occurred early the next morning, when General zu Bärenbaum entered my room. This was exceptional in itself, for the commandant never entered anyone's room—he sent for them. Pacing excitedly up and down, he cried, "Skrik, I'll be in your debt till the end of my days! Lydia speaks of nothing but you, Skrik. Her newfound compliance has ensured that my bloodline will survive. I owe this happy turn of events to you!" He clasped me fiercely to his breast and hurried out of the room, but not before I noticed he had tears in his eyes.

More tears flowed abundantly in the next few days—to wit, whenever I had to refuse one of the ladies an appointment at the time she wanted because another had already booked it. In no time at all, my appointments book was full two months in advance. I worked in a kind of trance, and the days flew by.

Then my activities extended to the nights as well.

Although I was only vaguely aware of them, it had not escaped me that executions were carried out in the barracks, usually at dawn. I had often been awakened by a volley of rifle fire and later seen a cart drive out of the barrack square laden with a coffin and followed by a priest with bowed head. One day, a lieutenant informed me of the commandant's decision that I would henceforth give criminals a final haircut on the eve of their execution. It seemed that the man to whom this task had fallen previously, a blacksmith from the local village, had died. It must be said, alas, that many condemned men had been dissatisfied with his technique, and since this final haircut was the one with which the deceased appeared before God on Judgment Day, it was only fitting to entrust it to an expert.

My first condemned man awaited me the very next evening. I was conducted to his cell just as attendants carried in the plates on which his last meal was served.

The man was seated at the table, sinking his teeth in a turkey drumstick. "Take a seat," he said, indicating his bunk. "You'll have to wait a moment." It was poor coordination on the part of the authorities, he said, to send in a meal and a hairdresser at the same time. What was he supposed to do? If I cut his hair, his food would go cold; and if I cut his hair while he was eating, the hair would fall into it. The whole thing was a complete miscalculation.

I agreed with him and introduced myself.

"A nice name," he said, "a very nice name. I used to know someone called Skrok, which is almost the same." The man had been employed by the royal hydraulic engineering department: dredging, watermill permits, fishing licenses, things like that. Not an easy job—a lot of disputes, people going to court over a few pathetic yards of riverbank, and so on. He had made Skrok's acquaintance when a man who owned the forest adjoining his own claimed that a certain spring belonged to him. "He came to see me, just like that, and said the spring was wrongly marked on the map—said it was on his property." So he'd sent for Skrok and asked him to settle the matter. After all, he said, he was the biggest landowner in the district; no one could simply come and dispute the ownership of his spring. And what did Skrok do? He showed up with a platoon of surveyors, who tramped around his forest and finally found that the other man had been right—the spring was on his property.

He tossed me a drumstick. "These people can cook, I'll grant them that. They're lousy organizers but decent cooks. Help yourself to some croquettes. There are far too many, who's going to eat them all?"

He now applied himself to a knuckle of pork. He was a man who looked as if he knew how to eat. Not fat, far less obese—no, he simply looked like a person who enjoyed his food. He had sent Skrok packing, he said, measurements and all. One day, Skrok wasn't there anymore, and the royal hydraulic engineering department had to find itself a new surveyor.

The condemned man did not have much hair left. I was worrying about this while listening to him.

"Yes," he said, "I started to lose it early on—all the men in our family have lost their hair at an early stage—but I've still got a few hairs left, and I'll entrust them to you when we've finished eating. I'm sure you'll make the most of them." Would I like to hear his opinion? Hair loss came down to these confounded wigs. Not only did you sweat under them and the lice grew as big as houseflies, but they made you look like a goddamn priest. When he inherited the estate from his late father, the first thing he did was send for the wigmaker, a conceited fellow who wore high heels, and tell him he was tired of looking like a goddamn priest, so he'd better think of something different.

"A few weeks later, the fellow turned up—Wockenfuss was his name—with a new assortment of wigs, and what can I tell you," he said. "They looked just like the old ones." He had sent Wockenfuss packing, wigs and all.

He pushed the plates and leftovers together. "Do your worst," he said, and leaned back. I went around behind him and gave his sparse hair a careful brush, wondering how to style it for Judgment Day.

He had always been a good father, he said. Tomorrow, when he came before the Heavenly Father, this was something that would undoubtedly count in his favor. His son Harald, for example, his first-born and heir to his property, was either obstinate or at least of limited intelligence, but the condemned man had always stood by him. Teachers had shown him exercise books in which Harald was supposed to do his homework, and they were full of doodles and obscene drawings. Could the teachers prove that they themselves weren't responsible for these? he had asked. No, of course they couldn't. Harald's French teacher, Monsieur Elouard, had been particularly impertinent. He suggested that the father attend a lesson to convince himself of the boy's obstinacy. The man had sent Monsieur Elouard packing, obscene drawings and all.

Having begun by brushing his hair into a clump on the top of his head, I moistened the tips of the hairs and twirled them into little spikes.

"You proceed systematically, it seems," he said. "I like that." He had fought against incompetence and disorganization all his life. It was no accident that his forests had become the biggest integrated property in Westphalia, given that he pursued a policy of methodical, farsighted consolidation. Noblemen, those feebleminded descendants of marauders and extortionists, were to blame for the ruinous state of the country. He had often sent letters to the king, explaining that his day was done—that he and his kind should bow out and hand over the affairs of state to men like himself. He had never received a reply. Never, that is to say, until three months ago, when he was invited to a discussion. Apparently, the authorities were interested in his views and his managerial methods.

He had never set eyes on the king. Instead he was arrested on arrival, charged with lèse-majesté, and sentenced to death.

He asked if I was finished, and if he might inspect his haircut. There was no mirror in the cell, unfortunately, so I gave him a verbal description of his appearance. He pronounced himself satisfied and regretted that we had not met sooner.

The morning after the execution, I learned that he had refused the priest who was to accompany him on his last walk to the gallows and hear his confession. He said he had already said all there was to say and had nothing to add.

A week later, when I again entered a condemned prisoner's cell, I stopped short. No one had told me that a woman was awaiting me in there. She was seated with her back to me, her blond curls falling gracefully to her narrow shoulders, then gathered with a black velvet bow and ending in a braid. When I came up behind her, she gave a start and sprang to her feet.

The prisoner wasn't a woman but a tall young man with a longish face, a long nose, and a prominent Adam's apple. He had long eyelids and long lashes—everything about him was long, including his body. He was a head taller than I.

He said he must have fallen asleep and apologized for his discourtesy. I had come to cut his hair in preparation for tomorrow morning, I explained, whereupon he quickly stepped back and raised his arms defensively. No, he cried, that was out of the question! After all that had happened to him because of his hair, he could not agree to it.

I bowed, wished him a pleasant last night on Earth, and turned to go. At the door, I paused and asked if his wonderful curls were natural or the product of a hairdresser's artistry.

"You like them?"

"I never saw any more perfect."

A tear welled in his eye. It hung on his long lashes for a while before trickling down his cheek. "Please stay," he said.

We sat down at the table. He had not touched his supper and asked me to try some. One should not eat much at night, he said; rich food was the root of many evils. It resulted in insomnia, constipation, heartburn, a bad complexion, and bad dreams. And hair loss. He welcomed my interest in his wealth of curls, which had delighted people since his childhood. When other infants were still toddling around with their heads entirely hairless or adorned with a few uneven tufts, his mother was already sitting beside his cot every night and brushing his silky curls. She assured him it didn't matter that he was the eighth boy she had brought into the world instead of the girl she had wanted, as long as he had such lovely hair. She did not believe that a daughter could ever have had more beautiful hair.

His mother's wish for a daughter was granted after all. Some years later, she gave birth to a girl with bristly black hair.

Jeremiah—that was the condemned man's name—told me that he was as smitten with his sister as she was with him. The more his mother spurned the little girl because she failed to match her expectations—she was stocky, thickset, and almost neckless—the more she idolized her youngest son. She indulged his every whim and employed the finest tailors to make his clothes, which he very quickly grew out of. Although he sensed it displeased her, she permitted him to spend nearly all his time with his sister. "I carried her around, fed her, and bathed her, and it was my ears that heard the first words she uttered." And the little girl, whose name was Turka, talked a great deal once she started; in fact, she talked almost incessantly. Jeremiah couldn't hear enough of her prattling, and at night, when Turka had already been put to bed and his mother sat down to brush his hair, all he could think of was the morrow and the moment when he would once more hear his sister's beloved voice.

The two of them were seldom seen together outside the house except in church at Christmas and Easter, because their parents avoided exposing Turka to public gaze. The years went by, and Jeremiah continued to grow. He was soon taller than all his brothers and his father, who had made a fortune as a horse trader. Turka, by contrast, became increasingly thickset.

Then she suddenly died for no reason. She had foreseen this. The evening before the night on which she fell asleep forever, she said to Jeremiah, "I shall be dead by tomorrow." When Jeremiah relayed this to their mother, she pooh-poohed it. "Don't listen to her," she retorted. "Turka talks a lot, and most of it is nonsense."

Jeremiah's mother devoted even more time to him after Turka's death. She took to instructing tailors to make gowns for him. He must now take over his sister's role entirely, she told him—he must fulfill his mother's dream of having a daughter with long, silky hair. He also owed this to his sister, whose life had been meaningless from the outset.

So Jeremiah spent his days thinking of Turka in the care of his mother, who oiled, powdered, and combed his hair with growing devotion. He no longer left the house—his mother thought it best—except on the anniversary of his sister's death, when he sneaked off to the churchyard and held conversations with her.

He did this on the tenth anniversary of Turka's death, as usual. Arriving at nightfall, he brought her flowers and told her about the most important things that had happened during the past year, not that there were many: his eldest brother had been killed at Waterloo, a housemaid had to be dismissed on suspicion of having seduced his father and was expecting a baby, and their mother had developed an inexplicable aversion to gooseberries. Then Jeremiah set off for home, which he reached unobserved, or so he thought.

The next day, a village child was found dead—a boy of eight, strangled and stabbed—and Jeremiah had been seen hurrying through the twilit streets dressed as a woman, his long hair fluttering in the evening breeze.

The court was quick to pass judgment: it took less than a morning to reach the conclusion that no one but a creature like Jeremiah could have committed such a crime. His mother did not attend the trial, a decision with which the neighbors entirely sympathized.

After inviting me once more to sample his supper—I again declined—he cleared his throat at considerable length, then asked if he might ask a final favor of me. I didn't know if I was the right person, I replied, pointing out that I was only a hairdresser, not a priest. That was just it, he said; I was far better qualified to fulfill his request. Then he asked if I would cut off one of his curls and take it to his mother after the execution.

In the next few weeks, I dressed another seven condemned men's hair for Judgment Day: the innkeeper who laced his beer with liquid manure to lend it more of a tang, thereby killing three of his customers, had flaming red hair that grew down almost to his eyebrows; the highwayman who pushed his victims into a ravine—complete with their carriages, after robbing them—wanted a pudding basin haircut like Julius Caesar's, whom he regarded as the most important highwayman in history; the belt maker who had driven his rival for the post of master of their guild insane by smuggling ferrets disguised as armadillos into his workshop, where they caused a great deal of damage, wore a leather cap that he refused to take off until his final minute on Earth; the verger who brained the village priest with a stack of hymnals—he secretly coveted the parson's wife—then hidden him under the confessional until the poor man's presence was betrayed by the stench, had fur like a mole's on his head instead of hair; the quack who sold childless women a tincture consisting of his own bodily fluids, thereby contributing to the birth of deformed children, had a braid sprouting from his forehead; the manager of a theatrical touring company whose plays preached revolution wore his long hair pinned up and concealed beneath an outsize top hat in which he also kept subversive tracts.

All these men were mild-mannered in their final hours, forgave their enemies and parents, and expressed themselves willing to give me a lock of their hair so that, following Jeremiah's example, they could have it conveyed to the bereaved as a memento.

My last condemned man was a swineherd who loved pigs, and whose hair had adapted itself to its bristly surroundings. He was not much older than I, and when he looked at me with his little eyes, which were fringed with white lashes, I grasped at once why the animals had been so dear to his heart.

"Looking at the beasts makes me feel all peaceful inside," he explained. "They know what they're in for, and that they don't have long to live, but they've come to terms with the fact."

I too felt calm and relaxed when he looked at me.

His name was Johann, and his father and grandfather had been swineherds before him. They never owned any pigs of their own but tended those belonging to other peasants, and they spent the summer months with their charges in the forest, where there were plenty of acorns and chestnuts; and when they returned in the fall, the pigs were round-bellied and fat. It was inevitable, after so many weeks, that one developed a personal relationship with the animals, Johann told me. Conversely, the pigs accepted their swineherd as one of their own.

They were neither servile and obsequious like dogs nor arrogant and demanding like cats; they were friendly and helpful. On cold nights, man and beast slept together for warmth on the forest floor, not only snuggled up side by side but sometimes on top of each other. This was a service the pigs offered their swineherds, though one naturally had to beware of being crushed to death beneath their weight while asleep.

Johann had been with pigs from birth. He began by accompanying his father, but soon took over pig families of his own because the animals sometimes became confused if more than one swineherd went with them. Naturally it was unpleasant to have to take them back in the fall, knowing that few of them would survive the winter, but the animals' equanimity and their acceptance of the inevitable had taught him humility too.

He was acquainted with only a limited number of pigs, of course, but he assured me that no two animals were alike. One example of this was a boar that led its clan unerringly, even across dangerous terrain, and refused to let Johann take the lead. It would stand stock-still until he got into line and then, but only then, move on. Another example: a young sow that kept trying to climb trees in emulation of Johann, who occasionally shinned up a tall fir tree for a better view of the surrounding countryside.

And then there was the sow to which he owed his life. Once, when they ran into a pack of wild dogs that surrounded them, growling fiercely—and then attacked Johann, whom they identified as the alpha male—she emerged from the cluster of terrified pigs, stationed herself at Johann's side, and lunged at the leader of the pack. She sent him flying, but by the time he had slunk off, whimpering, several more of the dogs had surrounded Johann and were snapping at him. They too went flying through the air, one after another.

When he brought the pigs back to their home farm at the end of the summer and set off with his bundle, the sow followed him. It was no use, she couldn't be persuaded to turn back—and in his heart of hearts, he didn't want her to. They spent a few happy weeks together sleeping in a hollow, and when the first night frost came, the sow lay on him to keep him warm. They were found like that in the morning. Johann was charged with theft and bestiality and condemned to death.

I found it hard to trim the sprinkling of bristles on Johann's head into a worthy haircut. To be frank, I failed.

Johann consoled me, looking at me sympathetically with his piggy little eyes. He assured me that he had nothing to reproach me for, his haircut was just as it should be.

I slept badly that night and was wide awake long before the time when the execution volley usually woke me. But I didn't hear it. Silence continued to reign for the rest of the morning. I subsequently learned that Johann had been reprieved at the last minute.

# 14
## *God forgot about us long ago*

The storm was waiting for us where it always did. *Liberty* had passed the Canary Islands when we were greeted by its outriders. The water was black, the wind blowing white spindrift over the turbulent waves, which were not as yet particularly big. Gray clouds were scudding so close overhead, you felt you could have touched them. At this stage of the storm, the "overture," as Odysseus Hirsch used to call it, the ship still lay quite sedately on the water—heeling over at an angle, to be sure, but cutting through the waves without undue effort. I was standing in the wheelhouse with Odysseus, who kept picking up his telescope. Things looked different up ahead, he said; the dance would begin around half an hour from now. This time it would be a polka rather than a waltz.

It became a fandango—wild, passionate, and possessive. The introduction was a wave that reared up ahead of the *Liberty*, seemingly out of nowhere, and hovered there motionless for a while, as if assessing us, before its crest buckled and slowly overbalanced. For a few seconds, time stood still—not a breath of wind inflated the sails, which hung limp. Then the mass of water just ahead of our bow came crashing down. The ship shuddered under the impact, and everything disappeared into the savage uproar that engulfed us.

As I strove to regain my bearings with water gurgling all around me, I had a sudden vision of my cabin. I had quit it when the ship's bell gave notice of the storm and hurried to the wheelhouse, leaving everything behind. In my mind's eye, I saw the mirror smash and my combs and brushes, scissors and curlers go flying across the cabin. I had advised the customer who had come to have his beard trimmed, as he did every morning, to return to his cabin at once and tie himself to his bunk because that was the only fixed piece of furniture. He would be safe there, I told him. Then I left him to his own devices.

I felt the helmsman's hand grope for me in the foaming water—Odysseus himself had not been upended, because he always lashed himself to the binnacle before a storm. Grabbing the collar of my jacket, he hauled me to my feet. Scarcely upright again and still spitting out the water I'd swallowed, I saw another wall of water towering over the *Liberty*. This time it scored a direct hit on the ship's bow, which plunged downward, hurling me against the wheelhouse window.

The aforesaid customer, who had some of the fastest-growing sideburns I had ever trimmed, was an experienced transatlantic sailor. He had been shuttling between Hamburg and New York for years, he told me, and had several times been on the point of sailing in the *Liberty*, only to have something to prevent it on each occasion. He was doubly pleased to be traveling at last aboard the ship that laid claim to the most famous hairdresser afloat. He had no real home, he replied, when I asked where his home was—he lived on board ships, though he was always on the lookout for a home. The problem was, he didn't have a suitable wife. What was a city, after all? Bricks and streets weren't a home—not for him, anyway. He had several times thought he'd met the right person, but alas . . .

. . .

After the helmsman grabbed me and set me on my feet again, he pointed to the chart chest and shouted, "There! Get in and shut the lid. Stay in there. Hang on tight!" The *Liberty* was climbing the precipitous wall of the next breaker. "Go! Go! Go!" Odysseus yelled. Not knowing if he meant me or the ship, I just had time to see us reach the crest of the wave and go racing down the other side before I jumped into the chest. Then I lay there in the dark and listened to Odysseus singing at the top of his voice as he stood legs astraddle, clinging to the wheel with his head thrown back. He loved these occasions, he told me once. Roman gladiators must have felt much the same during chariot races.

The homeless customer, who I hoped was safe in his bunk by now, had admitted that his first crossing of the Atlantic had not been entirely voluntary. When he was twenty, his parents—dance instructors who had failed to keep up with the latest fashions, and whose dancing school was past its best—had betrothed him to a good catch. They told the parents of the girl, whose name was Julie, that their son would shortly be appointed dancing master to the king's daughter, a well-paid post with the prospect of admission to the most exalted social circles.

My customer, who called himself Adolphe Durand—I discovered later that he chose a different name for every crossing, but for the moment he was Adolphe Durand—told me that he had been a tolerable dancer but had known nothing about his parents' fabrication. He merely noticed very soon that his future parents-in-law were obsessed with getting an invitation to court and were counting on him to pull it off. He didn't think twice about this, however, because Julie claimed his full attention and conquered him with her charms.

Adolphe had developed an early interest in biology. Fascinated by the multiplicity of life forms in the animal and plant worlds, he kept asking his father why they were necessary—surely it would be sufficient if there were horses, cattle, and sheep as well as human beings; then we would have animals to ride, animals whose milk and meat we could consume, and animals whose wool would keep us warm. His father failed to provide him with a conclusive answer—his allusion to God's plan and creation didn't satisfy Adolphe.

So he had to go looking for an answer himself, and he homed in on it step by step. The process began one day in the fall, when he watched some rutting stags in a forest clearing. Soon afterward, he observed two dragonflies interlocked just above the waters of a stream, then a pair of hedgehogs gingerly and cautiously venturing into contact. Adolphe was shocked by the sight of several drakes pouncing on a duck and holding her underwater until he thought the poor creature would never survive. By degrees, he gained the impression that what mattered was to try out as many different forms of procreation as possible. At one stage, he went stalking armed with pencil and paper, and it wasn't long before he had recorded so many different forms of copulation that he began to believe it must be the whole point of existence and the secret of nature's infinite variety. Frogs, birds, fish, ants, moles, stag beetles—and occasionally even human beings who visited the forest for that purpose—showed him what was possible in this respect. His drawers filled up with sketches that recorded what he had seen, and that he instinctively never showed to anyone. He had the feeling that he was depicting an aspect of life that, though omnipresent, wasn't really there. When he started to sketch combinations of the many different alternatives—eels with eagles, foxes with trout, flies with martens, weasels with quail—it seemed advisable to him to keep his drawings under lock and key, especially when he included his own species in these variants.

The only person he told of his discovery was Julie, who made it easy for him. From the first day they met—on an outing arranged by their parents—she responded with enthusiasm to all he said and did. For instance, when he informed her of his belief that God had forgotten all about the human race and addressed some other issue long ago, she was speechless: that was just what she thought too. And when he remarked that cheesecake wasn't a dessert that went well with bean soup, she clapped her hands in delight: at last she'd found someone who thought exactly as she did! Was he also of the opinion that it was time to hand over government business to women and teach men how to have children? When Adolphe replied in the negative, she confessed that she also thought such a theory utterly mistaken.

The first time he showed Julie his drawings, she was silent for so long, he feared that one or another of them had offended her. But then she said they must get married at once; the scenes she was looking at demonstrated there could be no greater form of harmony between two people than that.

But getting married turned out to be difficult. Julie's parents, who had already invested a considerable sum in his parents' dancing school, drew attention to Adolphe's forthcoming engagement as dancing master to the king's daughter. Adolphe, who quarreled violently with his parents over this, was fully supported by Julie. The king's daughter had no need of Adolphe or any other dancing master, she said. Early one morning, having gathered his drawings together and stowed them in a suitcase, Adolphe appeared outside Julie's home, intending to elope to the New World with her. She had been expecting him.

From inside the chest, I heard the roar of the storm gradually subside and Odysseus's singing gain the upper hand. Shortly afterward, he lifted the lid and helped me out. Standing beside him, I surveyed the damage the storm had inflicted, which would take some days to repair. The mainsail was torn, several spars had snapped, and there was no sign of the deck chairs, which had been lashed down. The *Liberty* was still laboring, but her movements were confident, as was the helmsman's expression.

"That was the liveliest dance I've had in years," he observed, wringing the water out of his cap.

I hoped that my homeless customer was safe and sound, likewise the rest of the passengers, but there was no question yet of making my way from the wheelhouse to the cabins, for waves were still breaking over the deck.

Alphonse and Julie lived on Alphonse's drawings while en route to Bremerhaven, whence they hoped to sail to the New World. He showed them to prospective customers in inns and rooming houses—discreetly, of course—and they sold like hotcakes. Many of his pieces were now in biological collections, he told me proudly. They were not highly priced in those days, so he met the couple's living and travel expenses mainly by sketching interested parties in their favorite amatory positions. In many cases he worked from fantasies they confided in him; in others from the happening itself, which they permitted him to witness. Julie was also called in on occasion.

When they finally put to sea after three months, Julie agreed that it would be more romantic to travel in second class on the lower deck. He thought nothing of it at first when, during their daily outing on deck, he saw her chatting with a first-class passenger, a gentleman whose every statement she endorsed, assuring him that she shared his view entirely. She concurred when the man expressed the opinion that she would be better off sleeping in his comfortable cabin, and also when he suggested that her best plan on arriving in New York would be to set off for the Wild West in his company, nor did she contradict Adolphe when he informed her that he proposed to sail back to Europe on the next available ship.

Since he had sold all his pictures and could find no prospective customers for new sketches on board, Adolphe spent the return voyage worrying about his professional future. Before he could come to any conclusion, however, he made the acquaintance of Daphne, a widow in her prime who had just lost her husband and inherited his fortune. She had never liked America, she told him, and her one wish now was to go home to Duderstadt. Adolphe thought it entirely understandable that she should want to hear him tell her, again and again, how right her decision was, and she found it miraculous that he too loved Duderstadt better than anywhere else in the world. He was surprised how easily long-forgotten steps came back to him when he was dancing with Daphne. He remembered all the ones his parents had taught him, and it had been a long time since Daphne had felt as youthful as she did in his arms. When they returned to the Old World, he suggested that she go on ahead to Duderstadt while he invested her fortune as profitably as possible with one of the big Hamburg banking houses.

And so, without really having planned it, he had happened on his new livelihood. He avoided the term *confidence trickster* but assured me that he had since "earned" enough to be able to afford a new home anywhere in the world. But, as he'd already said, without a wife to go with it . . .

After another hour, the storm had abated sufficiently for me to leave the wheelhouse. My cabin really did look as I had feared, but many were in far worse shape. Some of the passengers were crawling along the corridors on all fours, looking for their nearest and dearest; others suffered from circulatory collapse. Second-class passengers had come up from below and were getting in the way of crew members trying to help.

Among those who had survived the storm unscathed and were making themselves useful was Alphonse Durand. I saw him mopping up vomit, replacing pieces of furniture, and comforting tearful children. At his side was Betty. She wholeheartedly agreed with him when he declared that it was situations like this that welded people together and enabled them to display their noblest attributes. They hurried over when they saw me and announced that they had each discovered a kindred spirit: it had taken this hurricane to alert them to each other's existence.

# 15

## *No end without a beginning—certainly not a good one*

On average, according to my calculations, 155 hairs grow on every square centimeter of the human scalp. Men usually have up to 20 more than women, and dark-haired people display the greatest density—red-haired people the least. It often happens, therefore, that a dark-haired woman possesses more hair than a red-haired man. Women have hair growing on more square centimeters of scalp than men, and so, despite the inferior density of their hair, they will generally have more of it on their heads. This is because they tend to let it grow longer, for it is a widespread fallacy that hair becomes denser the more you cut it. This assumption applies only to people with curly hair, which displays less density the longer it is. The same goes for beards. I have observed that long beards ultimately lose their density, which cannot be restored by subsequent trimming. But in this case too, importance in respect of general appearance attaches to density per square centimeter, which varies considerably. The aforementioned 155 hairs per square centimeter is only a mean figure, of course; growth density can range from 100 to 220.

Ironically, it was the passenger with the greatest growth density I had ever seen—I estimated it to be 300 hairs per square centimeter—who asked me, while I was washing his hair, if it was possible for someone to survive without a scalp.

The man had proved himself a hero during the hurricane. A group of weeping children had fled from second class with their parents and become separated from them, and he had soothed them by reading aloud from a book he had evidently written himself. At one point in the story, which told of a trapper in the Wild West who had been scalped by Indians but lived for many years thereafter, one of the children piped up and declared that this was medically impossible. His grandfather had told him, he said. The scalp wasn't there for hairs to sprout from, but to prevent the interior of the head from drying out. Even if, in the trapper's case, the scalp had been loosely replaced on the skull with a hat on top, this would not have done the trick. The boy felt sure that his grandfather—who was a dermatologist, incidentally—would be happy to provide the author with further information on the subject.

I was reluctantly compelled to respond to my customer's question with some questions of my own: had he ever tested the child's assertion, what kind of book was it, and what was his name?

He was traveling incognito, he replied, because his books were bestsellers back home and he was a well-known man. He was going to the New World on a secret mission no one knew about, just as no one knew that he had never been to America before, even though his books were set there.

Could he tell me what they were about? I asked.

Indians, he replied. He was a Wild West author, but one who was totally misunderstood. He had always written his books for the Indians themselves, as instruction manuals on how to live in peace and harmony with the white man. Of course, no Indian had ever read one of his books. Instead, readers back home lapped them up as adventure stories in which the Indians were regarded as feather-adorned accessories, whereas they were really the Chosen People. Except that no one had ever told them so, alas. That was why he was on his way to them now. As for the scalp question: until I, being an expert, could prove the opposite, he would continue to assume that the scalpless trapper was still alive to this day.

The Wild West author did not leave it at one reading. The suggestion that he continue to read to the children in second class came from the boy who had felt bound to correct him on the subject of the missing scalp. From then on, the author appeared down below early in the evening, and it was not long before his audience included adults as well. When word of this exciting diversion reached the upper deck, the first-class passengers asked not to be excluded, and they eventually agreed that the readings should be transferred to the saloon. Although it meant they had to tolerate the presence of passengers from second class, they accepted this because the stories proved so entertaining. The classes did not separate again until dinner was served.

Little by little, the author took to confiding in me while I was shampooing his hair and massaging his scalp before readings. The key to understanding God's plan for the world, he explained, consisted in the exodus of the Israelites from Egypt. If I cast my mind back to the day the sea parted for them, enabling them to escape from their pursuers, I must surely have noticed that the Bible's description of the opposite shore was very vague. Where had they landed? He was absolutely convinced that they had trekked across the seabed just where we were now sailing now: immediately beneath us, in other words. And they had gone ashore where we would land: in the New World! God's Chosen People had immigrated to America, so the Indians were the true descendants of the Israelites. God had consigned the world to their care; it was their task to pacify people and create paradise on

Earth. This they had already done in America. Unfortunately, however, shipbuilding had developed more quickly in Europe than among the Indians, so they had been *discovered* before they could complete their task. It was certainly no accident that Columbus had kneeled and kissed the sacred soil—he knew exactly where he had gone ashore. The discovery of gunpowder had likewise occurred too soon in Europe, with the result that rapacious Europeans had been able to inflict great harm upon God's Chosen People.

But this too was a part of God's plan. He had more than once subjected his people to terrible tribulations in the past, after all, because that was a proven method of binding them to Himself: first inspire fear and trembling, then deliver them from it.

Although the author described in his books how the Native Americans were reluctantly but fervently adopting Christianity, that was only a trick on his part to make Europeans believe that they themselves were the propagators of the Gospel. This was where his mission came into play. Since God could not have foreseen the development of shipbuilding and gunpowder, such things being unimaginable in His day, He had neglected to prepare the Indians for the arrival of the Europeans and remind them that they themselves were his Chosen People.

It was his task to remedy this omission, said the author. He was going to explain to them that the white man, however masterful he might appear, was only a dimwitted descendant of the Egyptians. He couldn't state this explicitly in his books, of course, but he thought that one or two Indians would get the message. What was far more important, however, was to wean them from the warpath and explain the responsibility that devolved upon them in their role as the Chosen People. He knew he had little time left in which to do this, because more and more Europeans were flooding into the New World—as evidenced by this crowded ship. But if the Bible had taught us anything, it was this: there was no end without a beginning—certainly not a good one.

The author's readings on board developed into an institution no one wanted to miss. In order to secure good seats, the first of his audience would turn up an hour before the show began. At that time the author would still be seated in my salon, having his hair done, because he had taken to appearing in different roles. When he appeared in the guise of the hero of his stories, the white man who loved the Indians, he would have his fair hair slightly waved. He would also wear a trapper's outfit complete with a beaver-tail hat and a long-barreled rifle adorned with silver rivets—a dummy, but impressive to look at. When he appeared as an Indian chief who had sworn blood brotherhood with the white man, he wore white linen trousers with colorful embroidery and a shirt to match, and he asked me to straighten his hair and tint it black. On one occasion, when he turned up dressed as a female Indian, he asked me a little hesitantly if he could dare appear before his audience in such a guise. I plaited him a braid, an appendage for which his hair was just long enough, and assured him that anyone who didn't know better would mistake him for a squaw. That reading was one of his highlights, and it led on future evenings to his audience turning up in fanciful costumes too.

By degrees, the readings mutated into miniature theatrical performances. For instance, a scene in which the white man—a role played by Pernille Jakobsson—lifted a rock to demonstrate his physical strength to the Indians. For want of a rock, Pernille hoisted a member of the audience into the air. On another evening, Urs Hütterli impersonated a cardsharp fleecing unsuspecting drunks with a marked deck while Vladimir Gospodin played lively airs on the piano and Betty danced a cancan. Second-class passengers were also recruited. On one occasion, a dozen of them appeared as dirt-poor farmers begging a malicious cattle baron, convincingly played by Camillo Dagorne, for land on which to graze their cattle.

The second-class passengers were now tolerated "up top" at other times of the day. People began to get used to them, and they were even permitted to cast a glance at the cabins in first class. Conversely, first-class passengers showed their faces in the communal accommodations "down below." Some were horrified, while others found the candlelit dormitory romantic. However, the first time someone asked permission to spend a night down there—it was Baumhauer the employment agent, who offered the run of his cabin in return—the captain stepped in. He declared that the fraternization occasioned by the Wild West author's stirring tales had gone a bit too far. If the shipping company found out, he would lose his master's certificate. He had nothing against Indians or second-class passengers—both were equally profitable, after all—but he could not permit the natural order of things to be disrupted, least of all on board his ship. The lacemakers invited him to a confidential talk, and after they had spent a while together in his private saloon, they were permitted to move into the employment agent's cabin, and the agent bedded down in second class from then on.

The Wild West author told me one evening that he felt his mission was well under way, and if he ever returned home, he would look up the grandfather of the cheeky little boy and settle the scalp question. Until then, he would assume that the trapper could survive without one. When he asked me to give him a realistic trapper haircut, I advised against it. He appeared instead as Manitou, who called the father of the white man's blood brother to join him in the Happy Hunting Ground, a part for which his exceptional hair density made him look particularly convincing.

# 16

## *Your hands, we need your hands!*

Among the most noticeable second-class passengers were the Basils from Lauenburg and their four children. The parents: tall, thin, wiry, ramrod-backed; the children: quiet, fair-haired, well-brought-up, attentive. They always walked in single file, Ernst Basil leading, then the children in order of height, then their mother. All six said a polite "Good day" to anyone they met. They had a dignified aura that contrasted with their simple, rustic clothing. The children dressed just like their father in white collarless shirts, black trousers held up by suspenders, and round black hats. The mother wore a gray dress and a bonnet that hid her hair. The Basils were never seen sitting down or standing; they were always in motion—walking sedately but purposefully in one direction or another. What interested the other passengers was not so much their appearance as the fact that Ernst Basil, who called himself Ernest, had already experienced America and even owned a farm in Minnesota. His motive in undertaking this voyage had been to collect his family, who had been waiting nearly ten years for him to lay the foundations of a new and better life in the New World.

He told me this after coming to my cabin to have his sideburns curled. They were in a pitiful condition—hardly worthy of the name—because he had been unable to attend to them for almost a month. He did not, however, complain in any way about the tribulations down below—no, all his attention was focused on the life that lay ahead for him and his family. He had rented out his parental farm in Lauenburg and, with his wife's consent, used the money to travel to America and acquire land and a house there. He had done both those things. He had even increased his modest assets by single-handedly growing enough grain to sell to parties of settlers passing through.

Holding up his hands, he said that if I ever had any land to plow, I had only to let him know. He needed no pickax or shovel to render soil cultivable; his hands did duty for any kind of implement. He had very seldom used an ax or a hammer.

I had to admit I had never seen such impressive tools before.

He had done his utmost to avoid any form of distraction, he told me, but without success. First because of the settlers, whose covered wagons crossed his land with increasing frequency; but also because of the Indians, who visited him from the reservation nearby.

Their first appearance had given him a terrible shock. He was down on all fours, planting corn, when a shadow loomed over him—a bear lurking behind his back, or so he thought. He crouched there motionless for minutes before venturing to glance over his shoulder. The Indian was wearing a shaggy fur, glasses without any lenses, and a top hat. "Your hands," he said, "we need your hands."

When Ernest rose to his feet and went to shake hands, the man inspected the extended hand and said in an awestruck voice, "They are even more powerful than people say. Now we are saved."

It turned out that the Indian village was threatened by a mountain torrent that had overflowed its banks and carried away several tepees and horses, and—alas—some children as well. The authorities had refused the Indians' request for help and had failed to supply the equipment they'd promised, so the tribe's hopes rested entirely on him, Ernest with the hands like shovels.

He speedily built a dam that prevented the water from causing further damage, and when it was finished, the water level dropped because the thaw was over in any case. Ernest, who was credited with this, was now lauded not only for his shovel-like hands but also for his magical powers. He was invited to be the guest of honor at festivities lasting several days. There was drumming, dancing, and feasting on baked bears' paws, the dam was celebrated with much whiskey, and Ernest was offered a squaw.

He naturally declined the latter gift, though not without praising his hosts' generosity and the squaw's pulchritude. This met with the Indians' total incomprehension. If the squaw was ugly, they said, they understood and could offer him another. They were at a loss and seemed genuinely dismayed, the young woman most of all, who was little more than a child and gazed at him in despair. So he eventually accepted her, with thanks. She now lived in a shack he had erected beside his house, together with their four children, whose names—she had insisted on this—were Ernest Two, Ernest Three, Ernest Four, and Ernest Five.

He sighed deeply and raised his hands in resignation. How, he asked me, was he to explain all this to his wife, who knew nothing about it? But that wasn't all: he had later been obliged to erect three more shacks for another three squaws. On one occasion he had rescued the chief's horse, which had fallen into a ravine, by digging a tunnel through which the animal could be extricated. Another time, the Indian village had been threatened by a landslide when an avalanche of mud caused by days of rain had cut it off from the outside world. For neighborliness's sake, he had made no attempt to decline the squaws he was offered at the subsequent festivities held to celebrate his rescue operations.

His Indian neighbors were extraordinarily friendly, he said. It wasn't long before the squaws' mothers, who were now on the scene the whole time, politely but firmly gave him a nudge when one of their daughters was not expecting. And when he told the chief about his forthcoming journey to Lauenburg to collect his family, the chief offered to go in his place so that Ernest could continue to devote himself to his familial duties. He had difficulty in talking the man out of it and had to promise to make up for lost time after his return.

Now he was really in a fix, he told me. He had realized, even on the way home, that he would have trouble finding the right words to explain the situation plausibly to his wife. To be more precise, he still hadn't brought himself to do so.

Helena Basil, who had complied with her husband's advice to call herself Helen from now on, that name being more suited to America, came to me to have her hair done the following day. Helen and Ernest—she liked that, she said. They had also Americanized their children. Jakob was now called Jack, Gerhard Gerry, David Dave, and Benjamin Benny. After ten years away, she said, her husband had returned to Lauenburg an entirely new person. He used to be hesitant and positively timid, sensed obstacles and injustices everywhere, and avoided self-assured people; now he was filled with initiative and optimism and never at a loss for an answer to any problem. Only one of his former attributes had strengthened: his profound religious faith.

Had I noticed the sideburns he'd grown in America? When she asked about them, he said something about Mormons being numerous in the area in which he had built their family home, and added that he felt strongly drawn to those God-fearing folk and their way of life. She wasn't quite sure what he meant and wondered if I had any experience with Mormons.

Well, I said, for one thing, there was their typical hairstyle and uniform clothing; for another, they practiced a special form of family life. Generally speaking, several women gathered around a man they thought particularly capable of guaranteeing them a livelihood. It was much the same with certain apes—not that I was drawing a comparison between the two. Mormons attached great importance to education and good manners.

She said nothing for the rest of her appointment, apparently lost in thought. When leaving, she said—more to herself than to me—that education might prove a problem in these circumstances because she couldn't read or write.

The same day, Ernest Basil turned up and asked if I could spare a few minutes. After her visit to me, his wife had told him she wanted to learn at least the rudiments of reading and writing before they got to Minnesota. She thought that this would make a better impression on the Mormons living there and enable her to fit in more easily. He was touched by her plan, but at the same time, this development made it even harder for him to explain the situation. Above all, who would teach her, considering that he was equally unable to read or write?

That was irrelevant, I told him reassuringly. He must surely have noticed that the Indians didn't read or write either—not in the way we commonly do. The only things they ever put down on paper were circles, dots, and lines. It was simply another form of writing, and one that he, his wife, and their children would find it easy enough to learn.

He thanked me, looking relieved, and when Helen Basil visited me the next day, she too appeared to be easier in her mind. She was so proud of Ernest, she told me. Modest man that he was, he had only just confessed to her that he was regarded as a kind of mayor by the Mormons of Minnesota. Some of them had built houses in the immediate vicinity of his own, in which she herself would soon be living. These were considerably smaller—so small, in fact, that most of them were occupied by wives and children only. This presented no problem because the husbands spent most of the time away on business. It was one of Ernest's duties to look after their wives and children on such occasions—in other words, nearly all the time. This would not, however, affect their own family life in any way. She only hoped that the husbands didn't get the wrong idea, because one knew how readily men who are often absent tend to mistrust their wives' fidelity.

I then heard from Ernest Basil that his wife had made a surprising suggestion. Since there were Mormon families in which several women were married to one man, there must also be men for whom no woman was available. She suggested that, while the married men were away on business, these bachelors should be instructed to look after the grass widows during the day and sleep in the Basils' big house at night. The advantage of this would be that when he, Ernest, went away on business, she would feel safer, because he had told her that there were also Indians in the area—and what some Indians were capable of was apparent from the Wild West author's readings. Ernest's assurance that such Indians would never venture near a mayor's house had prompted Helen to suggest that the grass widows too should overnight in the mayor's house for their own safety.

The next day, Helen Basil had some news for me. Ernest had been so taken with her suggestion that he was considering building a new and far bigger house in a different spot—one that would accommodate numerous residents with ease. And since he wasn't altogether satisfied with the soil in Minnesota—too sandy, too stony—he was considering moving far away and starting afresh, preferably on the West Coast. Aside from anything else, the mayor's duties were taking up too much of the time he ought to be devoting to his farm. He had already made a sketch of their future home: a thatched, half-timbered house like the one they'd owned in Lauenburg. Would I like to see it? Eyes shining, Helen handed me a sheet of paper. I couldn't refrain from praising the sketch. It was a really handsome house, comfortable and manageable; possibly a little small for a couple with four children, but with plenty of arable land and a lot of fruit trees. Helen left my salon looking more elated than I had ever seen her.

The next day, Ernest asked me to cut off his sideburns, which weren't, he said, appropriate for a man like himself, who earned his living with his hands and loved his wife more than anything else in the world. He looked thoroughly relieved.

# 17

## *Even the strongest physique demands its due*

My visits to the officers' wives introduced me to all manner of grand apartments and many an unusual situation. This was because, although they valued my skill as a hairdresser, most of the women hardly noticed me. There was no reason why they should have. I was still a youth—on the verge of adulthood, it is true, but a nobody who took orders from their husbands and was kept at the barracks more or less against his will.

So they behaved quite uninhibitedly in my presence. Many received me in their negligees, while others wore face masks or consulted their lady's maids on what to wear, compelling me to interrupt my work while they tried on one gown after another. It also happened, while I was there, that they received their lovers, who urged me to hurry. One of them espoused the sensible view that it was pointless for me to do his lady's hair beforehand, so I had to wait while they disappeared into the bedchamber and was only able to complete my work thereafter.

I noticed, after a while, that many of these gentlemen paid visits to more than one lady. There was, for instance, one handsome young man whom I encountered at the homes of four different officers' wives. Notable for his exceptionally refined manners, he always brought them flowers and spoke softly, usually in French. The ladies laughed out loud whenever he whispered something in their ears, so it seemed he was witty and amusing. He was called Armande by Frau von Zitzewitz, François by Frau von Rosenbruch, Fou-fou by Countess Bülow, and Jean-Baptiste by Baroness zu Kerssenbrock. The last of these ladies used to bid him farewell with the words "Woe betide you if you're ever unfaithful to me!"—whereupon he winked at me. I inferred from this that he had taken note and knew what I knew.

This assumption was confirmed when he bumped into me outside the house of one of these ladies as I was on my way back to the barracks, and asked me bluntly which of them I liked best. Amused by my embarrassment, he draped an arm familiarly around my shoulders and informed me that he had decided to invite me to the nearby inn for a beer—if I could spare the time.

I was not a little surprised, on entering the tavern, to see several young gallants I recognized seated at the tables inside, eating. It was clear from their lively conversation and laughter that they were having a good time.

"We break for lunch," said Jean-Baptiste. "Even the strongest physique demands its due."

When we sat down, the young gentlemen nodded to me as if I were an old acquaintance. And I suppose I was, for Jean-Baptiste, who confided to me that this really was his favorite *nom de guerre* and I was welcome to call him by it, told me that of course they all knew me and valued my work highly. The only trouble was, the time at which I performed it was not always ideal. He felt sure I had noticed this, but there was no help for it, because the ladies always requested their services in the mornings, as they did mine. He ordered the braised beef and advised me to do likewise. It was excellent, he said.

I learned during the meal that some twenty young men were currently "doing business" in the garrison town—if I would pardon the expression. The relationships between them and the ladies were very personal, of course. They sometimes bred genuine emotion, which could result in awkward situations, but ultimately their livelihood was at issue—their business, in other words. They were not paid cash on the nail, of course—that would rob the affair of all romance. The ladies' maidservants brought them their fees, often to this very tavern, where they also transmitted any special requests or requirements their mistresses might have.

The braised beef was truly delicious, and when we parted, I resolved to visit the tavern more often on my afternoons off. On those occasions, I gradually got to know the young gallants better. This could lead to awkward situations—for instance, when we met in some boudoir the next day and avoided greeting each other like old friends. In the tavern, I learned more details of what went on in the garrison town: for example, that the ladies engaged in a lively exchange of views about their morning assignations and would consequently send their servants to request the services of certain gentlemen about whom they had heard good things. This did not, however, mean that they changed their swains daily. No, most of them had their firm favorites. For example, Frau von X—I'll mention no more names—had special predilections in which Lieutenant A (better to preserve discretion here too) was the expert. Countess Y took up a lot of time because she liked to act coy and be conquered with difficulty, whereas Baroness von Z was very quickly satisfied and Madame XY sometimes needed rough treatment, a technique for which Captain B was predestined. It was particularly difficult when wives requested two or even three gentlemen at the same time—difficult because they each had to simulate the appearance of a lover keeping a secret assignation. The best plan in such cases was for the gentlemen to turn up in quick succession, one after another, and angrily demand satisfaction from their immediate precursor, after which it would be the lady's task to settle the dispute to the satisfaction of all.

My hairdressing skills were making good progress at this period. After a rather expressive phase during which I allowed my imagination free rein or gave practical expression to coiffures designed with the aid of grass models, I now learned to develop creations that were more expressive of character or circumstances. Once I became acquainted with my customers' personalities, I might cease to be satisfied with my most recent work.

This happened in the case of Frau zu Granzow, whose hair I had initially dressed in a frivolous, almost fanciful manner, and whom I later perceived to be an extremely down-to-earth, tomboyish person. So I altered her appearance to accord more closely with her personality, and she remarked on looking at herself in the mirror afterward that she felt she was seeing her true self for the first time. The difference consisted mainly of the fact that I had plaited her previously piled-up hair into nine braids that stood out around her head.

With Baroness Friedenau, the opposite applied. At first inspired by the rather rustic lack of sophistication her awkward gestures conveyed, I subsequently realized that she was still inhabited by the dreamy little girl she had once been—who was, in her imagination, at home in an elfin, fairy-tale world. Her new coiffure, which was inspired by an onion dome, caused her to clap her hands in delight.

Something else that did a great deal to promote my development as a hairdresser was connected with the gentlemen's visits, though one thing governed the other: my presence shortly before their assignations made it possible for the ladies to prepare to play certain roles, which in turn required me to be versatile enough to help them achieve this. For instance, when Madame X—I will again be discreet—experienced a spontaneous desire to keep her tryst in the guise of a stable boy, or when Frau von Y wished to impersonate a female camp follower, this meant I had to improvise with equal spontaneity. Although these challenges occasionally brought me out in a sweat, I thoroughly enjoyed them. Strangely enough, I never had the slightest doubt that I would succeed in devising and accomplishing the right solution. I was told by Jean-Baptiste, with whom I was soon on cordial terms, that my involvement in the "business" had opened up new dimensions of pleasure for all concerned.

Another such dimension, though one that was to prove disastrous to me, stemmed from an occasion on which I had not completed my work by the time the lady's visitor arrived. Her eagerness was such that she was loath to keep her paramour waiting, so I was blindfolded with a black cloth and requested to continue my work while she devoted herself to him. This new experience of "blind" hairdressing put the finishing touch on my training—which I occasionally perfected still further by experimenting on grass models with my eyes bandaged—and soon became known to my lady customers, with the result that I was more and more often employed in this way.

Disaster struck on the morning when Lieutenant von Basedow came home unexpectedly. I never discovered why, but one of the chambermaids suddenly, without knocking, dashed into the bedchamber and cried, "Your husband, madame!" Initially believing this to be another piece of stage management, I was surprised to hear a loud commotion as the gentleman visitor hurriedly left the house via the balcony. Thus the lieutenant found his wife and me in circumstances that, in his unfavorable estimation, left no room for doubt. I was promptly arrested.

General zu Bärenbaum sent for me on the seventh day after my arrest. I had spent the intervening time locked up in my room, having been told that I was spared prison because there was insufficient evidence against me.

Circumstances seemed to have changed. I stood in front of the general's desk, hands manacled behind my back, while he paced silently up and down, likewise with his hands behind his back. Each time he passed, he paused for a moment and eyed me sadly. At length, he heaved a deep sigh and sat down heavily in his chair. Rumors about the wives of certain of his officers had been circulating for some time, he began—allusions to goings-on that defied his powers of imagination—but it had never occurred to anyone that I might be involved. Extensive inquiries having been made, and the household staff of the persons concerned having been interrogated during the last few days, the ladies had confessed, one after another. I could have no idea how disappointed in me he was. I had been something akin to a son for him, a son of whom he had been proud and who had even proved beneficial to him in his own marriage. He must now regard me in a different light, however, although his wife was not among those who had incriminated me. From now on, I would await my trial in prison, and he would do his utmost to see that the proceedings opened as soon as possible. My crime was too heinous for them to be delayed. I should consider myself fortunate that the soldiers he had assigned to guard me were not among the injured parties, for some of his officers would only too happily have taken the matter in hand themselves. Although he could not guarantee that they wouldn't do so, it was incumbent on him, as commandant of the barracks, to guard against that possibility.

My time in prison proved far from restful. The ordinary private soldiers assigned to guard me were bursting with curiosity and bombarded me with questions about the ladies. They pictured their assignations with greater powers of imagination than anyone would have credited them with, so I had little need to amplify. I did not answer their questions gratis—my quid pro quo consisted of their bringing clumps of grass and some of my equipment to my cell, so I was soon surrounded by a substantial number of coiffures that documented the progress I had made. My work had transcended its youthfully impetuous phase, I suppose, because these creations already evidenced the seriousness of adulthood and a creative awareness that would characterize the whole of my subsequent work. I refrained from working with my eyes bandaged and never did so again.

Several days and nights went by—not that I could tell them from each other because my cell had no window—so I didn't know how much time had elapsed when one of my guards informed me of developments in the commandant's office that obviously had some connection with me. It was only a rumor, but he'd heard that a French-speaking, high-ranking officer of the Royal Guard had appeared and was discussing my future with the general. Clearly, a higher authority was interested in putting me on trial.

Sure enough, I was brought before the commandant the following day. He was seated wearily at his desk while a tall man in a gorgeous uniform and a white powdered wig stood at the window with his back to the room. I was to be informed of something, said General zu Bärenbaum, and handed over to his visitor. Without turning around, the latter informed me that I was facing grave charges arising from my time as an itinerant hairdresser, and they were more juridically relevant than the crimes of which I stood accused here—among them trespass, theft, the pollution of public buildings, slander, grievous bodily harm, fraud, harassment of churchgoers, nocturnal disturbances of the peace, forgery, sacrilege, impersonating an officer of the state, offenses against public decency, cruelty to animals, calumny, perjury, poisoning wells, and forgery. For that reason, I would tonight be transferred to a prison under royal jurisdiction to await trial. In view of the tense situation in the barracks and the threats to my life, he and the commandant had agreed to keep this transfer a secret. To avoid arousing attention, he would come to collect me on his own at midnight. Then the man, who had spoken with a strong French accent, turned and eyed me sternly. It was Jean-Baptiste.

In the days that followed, which I spent hiding at a farm outside the garrison town where Jean-Baptiste had taken me, I learned that everything had changed there after my arrest. Jean-Baptiste told me that all his comrades had decamped at once—he too, of course—and taken refuge at his uncle's farm. That was where they had concocted the plan that had brought me there. But this could not, of course, be the end of the matter. There was also a carefully devised plan for me to escape to a place where I would be safe from the infuriated, cuckolded officers: America. They had collected enough money for a ticket and would escort me to Bremerhaven in the next few weeks.

And that was what happened. Naturally I was not escorted by all the gallants at once. They had organized a sort of relay system: I was to be handed on from one place to the next, where friends would secretly arrange overnight lodgings for me. This was a point of honor, Jean-Baptiste told me. He said it was not uncommon for one of their own number to get into similar difficulties, whereupon the network would go into action likewise. Although I wasn't a member of their guild, so to speak, they had taken me to their hearts and would do their utmost to ensure that I left the country unscathed. I had no need to thank them, let alone pay them. On the contrary—he and his friends knew me to be someone who had selflessly accepted his fate in order to protect others. One didn't come across that sort of solidarity every day of the week, and he would never forget me.

They all turned up the night I left my hideaway and set out on the first stage of my escape. Each of them gave me a hug and asked me to write from America to reassure them that I had arrived there safely.

# 18

## *We love being clouds!*

After five weeks at sea, the mood on board improved, becoming positively euphoric. The *Liberty* had now covered the greater part of her voyage, and if the winds remained favorable, she would reach New York in around two weeks' time—reason enough for passengers whose gaze had been focused largely on the past to look to the future. Their conversations now centered less on their old homes and what they had left behind than on what lay ahead, which began to come to life and take shape in their mind's eyes with increasing clarity. I recognized this shift—it was the same on every voyage, but this time especially so. The Wild West author's readings had undoubtedly contributed because they conjured up an attitude that corresponded with what the passengers hoped for from their future in the New World: brotherhood, public spirit, love. They exchanged mutual encouragement and advice, promising to keep in touch in America and help each other to the best of their ability.

Particular attention was aroused by a lady passenger who had seldom appeared in public until now, opinions being divided as to whether she was indisposed or merely unsociable. She announced the end of her seclusion with a piercing high C that silenced every conversation: Maria Tommasi di Bibione was beginning to ready her voice for the great tasks ahead.

Maria paid me her first visit that evening. She would be coming every day until the end of the voyage, she told me, because she had to get herself into tiptop condition both outwardly and inwardly. The former requirement she was entrusting to me. For the latter, she had found the perfect place: the compartment in which the freshwater casks were stored. Most of them had already been emptied, so they formed a wonderful resonator that would provide her with the ideal acoustics she needed to prepare herself for September 1, when she was to sing the lead role at the opening of the new Metropolitan Opera House in New York. She had terminated her engagement as lead soprano at Milan's La Scala especially for the occasion. Her agent, who was never wrong, had advised her to.

The latter, whose name was Guillermo Scalatti, was half the size of the opera singer and always stood silently one pace behind her, wearing a black overcoat and a derby. This applied even during her visits to my cabin. He closely watched every move I made and politely declined the offer of a chair.

The singer had discovered the rehearsal room herself after inspecting the second-class dormitory. She was very relieved that its occupants were allowed periodic respites from the stench of their cramped quarters. She had never seen worse conditions, except in the extras' quarters in the cellars of La Scala, where, having been hired off the street for a few lire, they had to wait for days during rehearsals because they never knew when the director would require their services. There were sometimes more than a hundred of them, and they gave off a pungent odor when they finally débouched onto the stage.

Serge, the ship's cook, who was in charge of the storerooms, had relinquished the freshwater compartment to her—so that was where she could now be heard daily practicing her scales and coloraturas, at first only in the afternoons but before long, just after sunrise. The result was that the second-class passengers appeared on deck early in the morning, still half asleep; and the other passengers, who found it hard to carry on a conversation, practiced forbearance for Maria's sake. The atmosphere prevailing at this time was one of solidarity, which obliged everyone to be magnanimous and tolerant.

Maria Tommasi di Bibione was exhausted when she came to have her hair done after practicing. Singing demanded everything of her, she told me—it exhausted her, and she had never enjoyed it. She had never wanted to become a singer at all, strictly speaking; never wanted to be the focus of admiration and veneration. Singing had taken over her life, and she had let it happen. Once the inauguration of the New York Met was over, she would leave it all behind her. She was hoping to find a suitable little place in America where she could indulge in her true passion: watching clouds.

Her career had been preordained. Her father, conductor of the fire brigade band in the little Tuscan town of Bibione, resented the probability that his trumpet playing would never be heard elsewhere—his musical talents had gained him that position only by dint of much effort and with the aid of family connections, his uncle being the mayor. He felt convinced that his lack of talent was due solely to his having bequeathed it all to his daughter. Maria's development proved him right: the results of the singing lessons she received at the age of three surpassed all expectations. With apparent ease, she overcame musical challenges that had defeated far older girls. Yes, she told me, it really had been easy, but a torment nonetheless. She had had to force herself to sing the whole time—for her father's sake—because music meant nothing to her. If he'd employed someone to teach her gymnastics or glassblowing, she would doubtless have learned them with equal facility, but she had never been interested in those things either. She had never confided this to a stranger before, she told me, but now, shortly before arriving in the New World, she felt the time had come. The truth was, she had never in her life been interested in anything but clouds.

Nevertheless, she demanded everything of herself during her daily practices amid the water casks. She practiced for hours on end, as everyone on board could hear, and her voice improved from day to day. Merely piercing at first, it became more nuanced. She imbued it with moods and emotions, varied its intensity from note to note, and conquered heights that attained the boundaries of what was audible to the human ear. And all this only by singing scales. When she began to sing ballads and arias, everyone on board realized that they were experiencing something very special indeed. La Tommasi, as they soon took to calling her, cast a spell over the passengers. Ones and twos came at first, then more and more of them gathered outside the door of the freshwater storage to listen to her from close at hand. The women on board, who were particularly moved, took to following Maria around everywhere.

That was why my little salon was soon thronged with ladies who, for want of adequate seating, sat down on the floor when La Tommasi was having her hair done. She told me that her father had spent all his savings—and, with his uncle's connivance, those of the town's exchequer—on singing teachers, though most of those musical pedagogues soon conceded that it required someone better than themselves to do justice to her unique vocal talent. So little Maria often changed teachers, people started to talk about her, and her name became well-known in professional circles even before she developed a bosom.

The women sitting at her feet exchanged meaningful glances. "A bosom," they repeated reverently. "A bosom."

But she had been self-assured enough to impose a bargain on her father: for every hour's singing lesson, he had to allow her ten minutes' cloud watching, or he would never hear her sing another note.

"Not another note!" chorused the women.

Maria started to record her cloud observations while lying down in the field behind her parental home and gazing at the sky. It seemed to her at first that the passing clouds were performing random maneuvers. Little by little, however, she discovered what it meant, for instance, when several small ones combined to form a big one, when they frayed and dissolved into nothingness, when they superimposed, overhauled, or engulfed each other. Every cloud's existence had a beginning and an end. Clouds conformed to a plan and knew what they were destined to do—that became clear to Maria as she lay there on the grass. Clouds were showing her the multiplicity of alternatives. They symbolized life, they had a message: *Look at all the possibilities there are. We enjoy being clouds, we love being clouds!* And Maria's love of clouds increased still more.

Her notes soon filled several of the exercise books she always carried, especially on cloudless days. That was when she went over what she had seen, and she saw this message: *Take the wind as it comes. Let it carry and mold you, whichever way it blows.*

Armed with what the clouds were teaching her, Maria was able to endure the increasing obligations that arose from her outstanding talent. She sang for princes and patrons, for eminent orchestral conductors and composers, and once for a dying prima donna who prophesied that Maria would be her successor. Her father engaged an agent—Guillermo Scalatti—who coordinated her growing number of engagements and knew how to make the most of her financially. It was he who had also arranged an audition at La Scala, Milan.

"La Scala, Milan," murmured her delighted admirers.

The audition caused a considerable stir, Maria reported. Not only because it was brief—the twelve-man committee rose after only three minutes and applauded her—but also because it was meteorologically successful. It had been raining for a week in Milan when she and her agent arrived, and the heavens were shrouded in dense, dark clouds. During the audition, the clouds departed, after which the sun shone down from an azure sky, the ankle-deep water in the streets began to evaporate, and people paused to watch the mist rising and dispersing around them. The connection was not recognized immediately, of course, even by Maria, because the audition had been held indoors—but when the director opened the French doors and escorted her onto the sunlit terrace, he exclaimed, "Your voice was heard in heaven!"

"In heaven," the women echoed, "in *heaven*!"

Even she had been surprised, Maria admitted. Although she had often wondered if there might be a way of establishing contact with her beloved clouds, none had occurred to her. She realized at that moment that her singing was the key. Under the director's astonished gaze, she stretched out on her back, looked up at the sky, in which a solitary white cloud was floating past, and hummed a melody. The cloud paused for a few seconds, then dispersed. Then Scalatti appeared on the terrace and told the director in a whisper that he wasn't to breathe a word about it, or she would sing at La Fenice instead.

Several years of vocal training began. Scalatti negotiated a contract with La Scala under which Maria would not be required to sing in public until she had developed a bosom.

"A bosom, a bosom!"

The contract also permitted her to watch clouds for two hours a day, during which time she was not to be disturbed by anyone. While studying the complete operatic repertoire, therefore, Maria also intensified her contact with the clouds. One afternoon, while she was lying on her back humming softly and imagining that a wonderful tumescent cloud on her left would alter course and draw nearer, the cloud did precisely that. It paused for a while, directly overhead, before moving on.

More and more melodies occurred to her after that, and they caused clouds to react in a wide variety of ways. She came to realize that her talent for singing had destined her to be more than an opera singer. Scalatti grasped this too.

During one exceptionally hot summer followed by a period of drought, Scalatti told her about the problems besetting farmers in Liguria, his own native district. He felt sure, he said, that Maria could solve them. He had made no promises, but it was at least worth a try. Maria thought so too, and they arrived there two days later, traveling by night so as not to attract attention. The next morning, she lay down on the parched grass outside Scalatti's farmhouse and started singing. Within a few minutes, the first clouds appeared on the horizon, and half an hour later the fields and meadows were soaked by a beneficial downpour. Maria and Scalatti left the village unobserved while the town's inhabitants were emerging from their houses and dancing for joy in the rain.

Scalatti thought it wiser to mention her gift to as few people as possible. Superstition was still rife, and it would be better not to expose her to it. The news must have spread, however, because more requests soon followed. Maria sang for a count in Bergamo who was anxious to irrigate his newly designed gardens; she sang for miners in Friuli who were threatened by landslides if the rain did not stop before long; she sang at the request of the city fathers of Lucca because the Arno had dried up after a long drought, and there were fears of an epidemic; and on one occasion she sang in Bibione to ensure the success of a concert by the fire brigade band for which her father had composed a march.

And then came her bosom. It developed at precisely the right time, Maria said, because she had just completed her study of the operatic repertoire. The director of La Scala deemed it an appropriate occasion on which to request Verdi to write a new work for Maria's first appearance, which would also be her introduction to Milan society. After meeting Maria, Verdi set to work at once, and four months later the new opera was ready. Rehearsals began, and the date of the premiere was fixed.

One week before that event, the Pope died. It had been raining in Rome for weeks, and no change in the weather was expected. It was centuries since a new pontiff had been installed in bad weather, and the faithful would construe this as a bad omen, Scalatti explained when he told Maria of the request he had received from the Vatican. The problem was, the announcement of the new Pope would coincide with the Scala premiere, and the director had quickly made it clear that there was no question of postponing the performance.

That first night surpassed all expectations. Roses were thrown onto the stage for three hours before the first note rang out. Verdi burst into a paroxysm of weeping when he heard Maria sing. The director announced that his career was over after the performance because he had nothing more to live for, and the firefighters from Bibione, who had been given complimentary tickets for the front row of the stalls, spontaneously formed a protective cordon to prevent hysterical opera fans from storming the stage.

The ensuing first-night party lasted until dawn, so Maria had to set out for Rome without a wink of sleep and doubted whether she would succeed in singing the city free of clouds. However, Scalatti reassured her by saying that, having already postponed the installation of the new Pope by one day, the Vatican would wait another if need be. That did not turn out to be necessary, however, so the Holy Father was able to appear on the balcony in brilliant sunshine.

"Sunshine, sunshine!" the women exulted.

Then Maria described the experience that would change her life forever. It was in her tenth year at La Scala. The opera on the program was *Così fan tutte*, and she guessed even before the curtain rose that something was about to happen. Everything went normally at first, but in the third act, she felt a melody take shape within her—one that yearned to make itself heard. Then, during the love duet, she could restrain it no longer. The melody she sang was not in the score, nor had she ever sung it before: notes and words of such beauty that they froze the conductor mid-movement and filled her partner, the wonderful heroic tenor Giuseppe Moronna, with unprecedented fervor. And outside, while she was singing, there gathered a storm whose thunder and lightning transformed the finale of the love duet into a preternatural manifestation. The people in the auditorium forgot to breathe for minutes—an omission that later, when the applause rang out, caused many of them to hyperventilate.

"Hyperventilate!" exclaimed the women.

It transpired the next day that all the lovers in Milan had felt close to eternity during those minutes. They had run out into the pouring rain and celebrated their love in the open. When the thunderstorm ended as suddenly as it had begun, many of them continued to roam the streets of Milan in a trancelike state for a long time afterward.

And she, Maria Tommasi di Bibione, knew that her art could never again be what it had been. From now on, she must place herself at the service of higher forces, for her power over clouds entailed a duty toward the human race. That, she said, was her true reason for immigrating to America, the continent of multitudinous clouds.

# 19

# *Those nudists are a blessing*

After circulating among the crew for some days, a rumor reached the passengers: a naked man was flitting around the *Liberty* at night, they whispered. Nimble as a weasel, he appeared sometimes here, sometimes there, and made no response when challenged. If approached, he vanished at once.

"The ship's hobgoblin," said Odysseus Hirsch when I buttonholed him and asked if he had seen the man while on watch at night. "Or Neptune in person. People start seeing all kinds of things toward the end of a voyage. Their brain invents them for want of anything really happening. It's an old story, Skrik." He himself had seen nothing of the kind, he said, and I also felt sure it was just the usual scuttlebutt.

The passengers formed patrols that ranged the deck at night. Come morning time, it would be reported that the man had been sighted again—that he had flitted past someone. Although everyone on board was soon in the know, the subject was discussed only in whispers for fear of frightening the children. After another few days, it was reported that the man had said something—a sort of slogan like "The day will come!"

Next, someone claimed to have heard the man say "Down with power!"—it might also have been "Now's the hour!"—in any event, everyone quickly agreed that he must be an anarchist. For some time now, it was said, the second-class passengers' suspicions had been aroused by one of their number, an odd-looking individual traveling by himself. Although he had not identified himself as an anarchist by word or deed, everyone knew how skillful anarchists were at putting on an act. That was their distinguishing feature.

Odysseus Hirsch bemoaned his lot to me. Gone were the heavenly peace of the night watches and the magic of cosmic infinity, with its glittering panoply of stars. Those patrols were now skulking around all over the place, he said, bumping into each other and knocking over buckets and tools in the dark. If they didn't capture this disembodied spirit soon, he would have to take the matter in hand himself. He didn't answer when I asked him how, just said it was probably a figment of the imagination anyway.

But then, one night, there was a commotion on deck. It seemed that a patrol had cornered the man, at least briefly. They had not been able to detain him, however, because he was not wearing any clothes they could have caught hold of. So he had made off—what was more, in the direction of the lower deck. There could be no further doubt: he was the anarchist.

The next morning, when a sheet of paper bearing the inscription "The time has come!" was found, action was taken. Two sturdy seamen fetched the man from his bunk and took him to the captain, who invited several experienced members of the crew to participate in his interrogation. They included Odysseus Hirsch; Serge, the ship's cook; and me.

The man, whose name was Oleg Krassimov, came from Moscow and possessed papers that confirmed his identity beyond doubt. He was impeccably dressed in a suit and tie, plus a hat he had insisted on putting on before being led away, saying that he owed it to the captain as a mark of respect.

To our surprise, he made no secret of his political sentiments. Yes, he said, he was an anarchist. He and some other members of the movement to which he belonged had been very badly treated in Moscow, and he was hoping to come across some of them in America. And yes, he was also a nudist, believing that way of life to be the only correct one, but he had never uttered a word about this to anyone on board, much less removed his clothes. He had been wearing this suit ever since we sailed, and he was longing for the moment when he could tear the clothes from his body—but he wasn't the wanted man. This was the very first time he had left the second-class accommodations; he felt sure he could find dozens of witnesses to that effect. When it was objected that most of the passengers were asleep at night and he could easily have reached the deck unobserved, he retorted that he also spent his nights asleep.

Since Serge knew Moscow well, he asked permission to question the man and took over the interrogation. Where had he lived as a child? Serge asked. The address seemed to tally, and, what's more, Serge knew the street. When he asked which school Krassimov had gone to, he found it to be one he himself attended for several years. They both had a vivid recollection of the school janitor, a former boxing champion who had secretly taught boxing to select pupils in the cellar.

That man had opened his eyes to the truth, said Krassimov. He had taught him that nothing in life was written in stone. Those who now held power and led a pleasurable existence at the expense of others, with their fur coats, carriages, and mistresses, were merely predators. They had simply taken whatever they wanted—none of their powers and privileges was God-given. Every individual was capable of altering the course of history. The power of the fist was the key to understanding the conditions prevailing throughout the country: oppression, exploitation, servitude. That was precisely what the janitor had taught him without uttering a word; his pugilistic skills had spoken for him. This was understood by all the youths whom that man had taught, and they had all had one sole objective thereafter: to change the world with their fists and give the oppressed their freedom back. Yes, he was an anarchist, and if we wanted to keelhaul him for it, we were welcome to!

We didn't keelhaul him, of course. We asked him to continue.

On leaving school, the youths, who were now young men, met in secret to plan their course of action. Krassimov himself was working in an iron foundry where, at his instigation, a boxing academy had been established because the management thought it a good way to toughen their workers physically. This inspired imitators, and boxing academies came into being in more and more factories. Not all the pupils grasped the ulterior purpose of their training, but this fully accorded with the instructors' wishes, because they had no wish to risk their schools' being unmasked as what they really were: germ cells for a new and better world.

Krassimov admitted that he and his comrades made a lot of mistakes. In their endeavor to prevent any power structures from evolving, they neglected to create an effective organization. Although the heads of the boxing academies met in secret, they failed to agree on a concerted plan of action; and since no one had the final say, no decision was made as to when the time would be ripe to strike. And when events speeded up, they became victims of their own lack of planning.

It began with the arrest of the janitor, who was accused of having held nudist meetings in the school cellar. When the news spread, everyone grasped that they couldn't afford a moment's hesitation: they must free the man who had taught them to understand the world, then free the world itself from those who had usurped it. Within a few weeks, more than a hundred trainee boxers were ready to seize power in Moscow. In full-dress uniform—i.e., boxing shorts and boxing gloves—they poured out into the streets and punched them clear within an hour. People sought refuge in doorways and churches. Then, when the boxers had run out of opponents, some soldiers came marching around the corner. They formed a circle around the anarchists and took aim. A sergeant-major presented them with two alternatives: lay down their boxing gloves or die in a volley of musket fire.

By nightfall they were all in a Moscow prison, where they met up with the janitor, who had already established a boxing academy supported by the governor for disciplinary reasons. Most of them were released within a few days, but the ringleaders—of whom he, Oleg Krassimov, was one—had been sent to a labor camp.

Serge said he still remembered that dramatic day. Although he was only a child at the time, he had been impressed by those intrepid boxers, who were wearing shorts on a day when the horse dung on the streets froze solid within seconds. He hoped that Oleg had done all right in the labor camp.

Oleg nodded thoughtfully. That was where he had learned the second lesson of his life, he recalled. Shortage of clothing had made it customary to work naked there. That was an advantage when cutting peat, felling trees, or building dams in the sweltering heat of the Siberian summer. More than that, however, this intimacy with the soil and the elements had convinced him that nudity was the only desirable state for him to adopt from then on. He had naturally been obliged to wear clothes when escaping from the labor camp because a naked man would have attracted too much attention, but now he could hardly wait to land in the New World and throw himself to the ground, naked at last. He dreamed of this in his bunk every night—surely that was sufficient proof that he could not be the wanted man?

Even so, it was decided that Oleg Krassimov should remain in custody for a few days until the agitation on board had subsided. He was locked up in a storeroom beside the opera singer's rehearsal room and assured that he would want for nothing.

The naked man was sighted again the following night.

"He's back," said Odysseus Hirsch when he woke me up, thereby rescuing me from a confused dream in which the *Liberty* had for weeks been becalmed off the New England coast for lack of wind—stores were running out, and passengers starting to jump overboard in hopes of swimming the last two hundred miles. The naked man was sitting in the wheelhouse and refusing to budge, Odysseus told me. I was an expert at dealing with difficult people, so would I please come and persuade him to change his mind?

The man was crouching on the floor of the wheelhouse, trembling. I asked Odysseus to let me speak with him on my own. I was about to introduce myself when he looked up and cried, "Skrik! At last!"

I had never seen him before. He was young and well built, with a full head of dark hair, and his body was extremely hirsute too. "You're cold," I said, offering him my jacket.

"The great Skrik," he replied. "They'll listen to you. Can I rely on you?"

First he would have to tell me what this was about, I replied, and didn't he want to get warm? Not yet, he said, declining my jacket. He was not doing this for fun but to help a friend, and for that he needed my help. I sat down on the deck beside him and offered him a cigarette. They had detained the wrong man, he said—Krassimov was completely innocent, and he had given himself up in order to prove it, because if the naked man continued to make trouble while Krassimov was locked up, he obviously couldn't be the wanted man. Oleg Krassimov had been his boxing instructor in Moscow, his idol, a man who would make the world a better place. He mustn't be incarcerated any longer—I must see to that now I knew who the naked man really was.

This seemed logical enough, but just then Odysseus Hirsch shouted, "Skrik, look! Another one." He pointed forward, and I caught sight of a naked man running across the dimly moonlit sundeck. He bounded into the air several times, threw up his arms, and disappeared from view. Odysseus dashed after him. The man beside me had risen to his feet. I asked if he knew who the other naked man was, but he said no, he hadn't known that there were any other Muscovite boxers on board. Then he asked if he might have my jacket after all.

When Odysseus returned, breathing heavily, he told me that the naked man had vanished, seemingly into thin air, after being chased all around the ship three times. Peering into the wheelhouse, he asked where the second naked man was. I said he had already gone below and would be returning my jacket tomorrow.

Soon afterward, when I was back in my bunk, my dream had a happy sequel: a horde of naked men surfaced around the becalmed ship and towed it toward America. There were thousands of them, their white bodies covering the sea as far as the horizon. The passengers lined the rail and urged them on. Those nudists are a blessing, they said; the world would be a poorer place without them.

The next morning, my jacket was returned by Krassimov's admirer. Dressed like his idol in a suit and hat, he asked if he might pay the prisoner a visit. I conducted him to the makeshift cell, where he remained for a long time. When he finally emerged, he informed me that he and Krassimov had a joint suggestion to make: in order to prove to the passengers and the world at large that neither anarchists nor nudists were to be feared, they were prepared to stage a public boxing match. They had the requisite equipment in their luggage and would consider it an honor to thank us in this way for the magnanimity we had shown them. Elsewhere they would have been summarily consigned to a labor camp, if not worse.

When I informed the captain of this proposal, a lively discussion ensued. The principal bone of contention was whether it would be proper to allow the pair to appear naked, as they suggested. Serge acknowledged that this would accord with the ancient world's notion of boxing. Odysseus, by contrast, thought it inappropriate because we were not in ancient Greece, where men had boxed naked only because boxing shorts were still unknown. The captain ruled that the contestants should wear not only shorts but undershirts, his contention being that exposure to sunlight at sea was detrimental to bare skin.

The passengers were electrified by news of the forthcoming event. The two boxers requested a week in which to prepare because they were out of training, so the fight was scheduled for eleven the next Sunday morning. During the days leading up to the bout, they trained on the foredeck, where the construction of a boxing ring had already started. They stunned onlookers with their demonstrations of shadow-boxing and skipping, performed push-ups and knee bends for an hour without stopping, and toughened their muscles by jumping on each other's stomachs in turn. During intervals in training, they told their astonished audience about their campaign against the fur coat–wearing oppressors of their native Russia, and about the anarchists' efforts to make the world a fairer place. They were loudly applauded.

As Sunday approached, the weather changed, becoming extremely wet and windy; but on the morning of the fight, the clouds parted and the sun shone down on the ring, which had been finished in time. The passengers thronging the foredeck formed an alleyway when the two boxers appeared and made for the ring, skipping as they went. They looked magnificent in their boxing shorts and their gloves, which resembled huge balloons. When they were face-to-face at last and ready to box, someone called out that there was no referee, and the fight couldn't start without one. The captain asked me to perform that function. I protested that I had never seen a boxing match in my life, but my voice was drowned out by applause. I had no choice but to climb into the ring.

Just as I was about to start the fight, the sun disappeared behind a bank of clouds and, to the accompaniment of peals of thunder, the ship was enveloped in a downpour such as I had never experienced before. The onlookers fled, and I called on the two boxers to do likewise, but Krassimov shook his head. He had not become an anarchist to be defeated by a drop of rain, he declared, and the two men proceeded to box.

The rain became steadily heavier, and the wind developed into a gale. I clung to the ropes to prevent myself from falling headlong. The two boxers, who were hurled to port and starboard alternately, tried to land wild swings as they staggered past each other, but they failed. Having made a last vain attempt to persuade them to suspend the fight, I left the ring and crawled into the dry indoors on all fours. I was soaked to the skin by the time I reached the saloon, where people were standing at the windows and peering out through a curtain of rain.

After the storm had subsided, both fighters were found lying senseless on the canvas. When they were carried inside and had recovered their breath, they dazedly but happily acknowledged the applause that greeted them. The passengers' admiration was boundless, and the anarchists' cause had received a considerable boost. The nocturnal nudist seemed to have been impressed too, because he was never sighted again.

# 20

## *People paid only as much in tax as they thought fit*

Certain women seem to be enclosed by a protective cocoon. When other women's coiffures are disheveled by the wind, theirs look fresh from the salon; when rain washes the rouge off other women's faces, theirs look more radiant than ever; and when the cold turns other women's noses red, theirs look freshly powdered. What's more, this does not apply to their outward appearance alone. When other women are forced to their knees by strokes of misfortune, they develop unsuspected strength; and when others despair of life's injustices, they fight and triumph over all adversity.

I met one such woman on each of my voyages aboard the *Liberty*, and I did so again on this, my last. She had shown herself to be a woman of that kind during a brief encounter on the day we sailed, when the female passengers got soaked. Her dignity and serenity had outshone them all.

Countess Urbach was not traveling alone. She was accompanied by two nieces and a trunk that she kept in her cabin. Everyone naturally wondered what she was transporting in the trunk—it was six feet long and fitted with numerous locks—but she never referred to it and nor did the young nieces, who always strolled the deck with her and escorted her to meals. When she visited my salon, they waited outside. Every now and then, one of them would put her head around the door, whereupon the countess would raise a reassuring hand and say she was fine, no need to worry. Her nieces were afraid she wouldn't survive the journey, she confided to me in a whisper, whereas it was the other way around: she was duty-bound to worry about her nieces, they being the last surviving members of her family.

The countess told me that the Urbach family owned such a large estate in the margravate of Brandenburg that it took four days to travel around it by carriage. Her husband had worked tirelessly to enlarge the estate in company with his brother. He was inspired by the idea of creating, on his own land, a community that would present a resplendent contrast with the wretched, arduous existence of the rural population in the vicinity. He aspired to be the servant of the farmers, millers, foresters, and agricultural laborers, male and female, whose customary lot it was to serve their masters and increase their wealth with the work of their hands. He held that service was the duty of the property-owning class, the task of those who directed the destinies of the community by virtue of their wealth and intelligence. That task must be performed for the benefit of those entrusted to their care, he believed, so he toured his estate unceasingly, getting to know all who lived on it, acquainting himself with their cares and concerns, and helping them to cope with life as best he could.

On one occasion, a flock of sheep was stampeded by a wolf and trampled their shepherd, who sustained several broken bones and was unable to work for some time. For want of anyone to replace him, Count Urbach took over the man's flock until he was back on his feet.

Another time, a gamekeeper shot himself in the leg while chasing poachers and would have bled to death had the count not gone looking for him in person and found him in the forest. Another notable incident concerned a miller's wife, who left her husband, a chronic sleepwalker, when he mistook her for a sack of flour and attempted to tote her into the local bakery. Count Urbach rode after the woman and changed her mind by promising to summon the finest available physician to cure the miller of his somnambulism. When he escorted her back to the mill, their route was lined by cheering villagers.

The countess told me that she herself had her hands full because her husband kept bringing derelicts home with him and putting them up at the castle, especially children who had lost their parents and poor old folk evicted by their families because they owned nothing worth inheriting. He provided them with clothing, food, and lodging. One pair of toothless old peasants spent a year living in the room beside the count and countess's own bedroom. Up until their very last day there, they both slept on the floor because they distrusted their soft feather bed and were afraid of suffocating in it.

The castle had resembled a hospital, an orphanage, and a poorhouse all wrapped up into one. The count was never happier than when every room was occupied. Having children of their own had been out of the question, the countess told me. Her husband's brother, Alfons, had at least found time for his wife occasionally—hence her two nieces. I mustn't misunderstand, though: she had loved her husband deeply. His loving care and compassion would probably have sufficed for half the world's population had he been left to his own devices, but he wasn't.

Their problems began when the landowners and nobility of Brandenburg addressed a petition to the district administration complaining that more and more of the agricultural laborers and artisans from their estates were moving to Count Urbach's, allegedly because the working conditions and pay there were better, but really because of the low taxes the count levied. Unless a stop was put to this, the whole of public life would be destroyed. Who would finance the livelihoods of property owners if there was nobody left to work for them and pay taxes? Count Urbach's machinations were undermining the social system and must be stopped at all costs.

A senior civil servant called on the Urbachs and requested a talk with the count—in private because publicity was undesirable, and he hoped to settle the matter amicably in view of the family's good name. Although Urbach County was the most flourishing district in Brandenburg, this situation could no longer be sustained at the expense of other landowners. The count must raise taxes and limit the preferential treatment extended to his workers and tenants in order to end this labor drain, which was beginning to resemble a mass migration.

Needless to say, neither the countess nor her husband gave serious consideration to this proposal. They did, however, promise to think it over and invited the civil servant to spend the weekend at the castle as their guest. He left the next morning after some demented old pensioners snatched his breakfast egg and refused to give it back.

Events speeded up in the next few weeks. For one thing, official letters arrived at ever shorter intervals demanding that the count shut down his social and charitable institutions forthwith. At the same time, he redoubled his activities in a way that even his wife found peculiar. He founded and financed cookery schools for unmarried agricultural laborers, advice centers for difficult mothers-in-law, drawing lessons for talented peasant children, and harp recitals in hay barns. People had to pay only as much in tax as they themselves thought fit. Since all the inhabitants of the county were in work and well paid, the population swelled still further. The influx was so great that reception centers had to be set up. The countess became patroness of these and spent most of her day there.

In order not to blight her husband's enthusiasm, she had kept the official letters away from him, so he mistakenly believed that the dark clouds had lifted. When the storm eventually broke, its impact was all the stronger. One Sunday morning, a detachment of the Prussian Guard took up its position outside the castle, and an officer demanded that the count offer no resistance. Legal proceedings against him and his brother would open on the morrow, and he had come to ensure that they attended the trial.

Countess Urbach had no time to explain things to her husband and tell him about the letters containing advance notice of the trial. She said she felt sure it was all a misunderstanding, for how could anyone call to account a person who was so beloved by those in his care?

He too seemed unconcerned when he informed the officer that he was willing to obey instructions for the sake of peace. He boarded a carriage whose door was locked behind him and waved to the countess through the window—her very last memory of him. He never reached the city, for he suffered a heart attack and died on the way.

The funeral of August, Count of Urbach, was a spectacular occasion. So many thousands of people gathered outside the castle where he was laid out in his coffin that his wife eventually opened the doors and allowed them to take their leave of him. They filed past his coffin for two days, and the commander of the Prussian battalion who was drawn up outside held off until the last of them had gone. He then occupied the castle and informed the countess that she must leave the country at once. That night, she resolved to travel to America with the coffin and her two nieces and bury her husband there. That done, she would return home and carry on his work.

# 21

# *Skrik Parties were held all over Boston*

My arrival in America after escaping from the infuriated army officers did not go as expected. A cyclone was raging off New York, so the sailing ship in which I had embarked at Bremerhaven—the *Gustav Nachtigal*—was diverted to Boston. That made no difference to me, but a young woman with whom I had spent a lot of time during the voyage was in despair, as were many other passengers. An uncle of hers in Berlin, who was in the American cotton trade, had secured a position as a maidservant for her in the home of a New York business acquaintance, and she was expected there.

Erika was nineteen years old, like me, and had no conception of America. She kept saying, "Erika in America—that's like Ina in China." She'd had a girlfriend in Berlin named Ina who knew all about China.

This girlfriend believed that names were inherently significant. Ina was actually in China right now, Erika told me, because her father was serving with the Prussian troops who had occupied Tsingtao. The

Chinese were a thoroughly ungrateful people, Ina had informed her. They refused to swap their tea for German lignite and did not want British opium either.

Erika was hoping that the Americans would prove less obdurate than the Chinese, and she wept because she was worried about her friend Ina. She tended to worry quite often, but she was just as quickly reassured.

I spent the voyage in second class, although the money collected for me by Jean-Baptiste and his comrades would have stretched to a first-class ticket. I thought it wiser to be thrifty and not land in America entirely without means.

Erika was in the same position. Her uncle had provided her with so much money that she was in constant fear of being robbed, and once we had gotten to know each other well, she asked me to hide her money under my mattress.

Men and women had separate dormitories on board the *Gustav Nachtigal*, but they ate together—soup was served twice a day—in a former storeroom converted into a dining saloon. That was where I first noticed Erika on account of her wonderful hair, which was thick and luxuriant and worn in a chignon.

It was on the road to Bremerhaven that I felt an incipient restlessness due to the fact that I missed cutting hair. It became painfully clear to me during those days that this was more than a passion: it was my elixir of life. The longer my hands were bereft of comb and scissors, the more my spirits ebbed. By the time I lay down on my bunk aboard the *Gustav Nachtigal*, I was so exhausted I slept for three solid days. The instant I caught sight of Erika's hair in the dining saloon, my desire to get at it was like a child's lust for a long-denied candy. I couldn't take my eyes off it.

The next day, while I was looking around for her, she suddenly sat down across the table from me and said, "You'd like to do my hair, wouldn't you?"

I nodded, and we spooned up our soup in silence. After the dining room had emptied—most of the passengers were taking advantage of their allotted hour of fresh air on deck—I asked her to wait for a moment while I fetched something from my suitcase.

She was already seated on a chair in front of the dining room's single porthole when I returned with my equipment. How did I propose to style her hair, she asked while I was draping the cape around her. That usually occurred to me when I had already started work, I told her; it was possible that my brain had already evolved a plan of which I wasn't yet aware. I asked her to unpin her chignon, and when her abundant brown hair fell loose about her shoulders, my hands set to work by themselves.

Although I heard Erika's voice only faintly because my ears were buzzing with happiness, I gathered that she was an orphan, the only child of a couple of church organists who had lost their lives in a coach crash. The horses had bolted because the pair was arguing too loudly over whether it was permissible to transpose a Bach cantata in order to play it on an Arp Schnitger organ. Her mother had been in favor; her father considered it unthinkable because the key had been chosen deliberately. He sang a short passage to demonstrate this, and he was repeating it a semitone higher when each horse bolted in turn and galloped into a wall. The coachman managed to leap off just in time. "You see what I mean?" her father cried triumphantly to her mother an instant before the coach was smashed to smithereens. Erika, who had been sitting behind her parents among some pieces of luggage, survived the crash.

Her maternal uncle's family took her in, but conversations about music were strictly forbidden after the terrible accident. This had a psychosomatic effect on Erika, who had never heard any other subject discussed before. She was then age five, and her attendance at school had to be deferred from year to year because she had lost the power of speech.

She was still moved today by the thought of her uncle's generosity and patience, she told me, but what she was most grateful for was his ingenuity in taking her to a recital at which Bach cantatas were to be played on an Arp Schnitger organ. When the piece her father had sung rang out, she felt speech well up inside her like a spring tide; and when the crucial notes were indeed transposed by a semitone, she asked her uncle, in a firm voice, to buy her an ice cream. He burst into tears and clasped her to him until the end of the recital. "She didn't die in vain," he sobbed. "My sister was right!"

Erika was the first woman whose hair I did on board a ship. She wasn't alone in approving of her new hairstyle, a slightly twisted cone whose shape lent it exceptional stability. Some other women came in while I was still at work. I dealt with two more that day, and I was busy from morning to night in the days that followed, there being more than fifty female passengers in second class. I charged them nothing; the fact that I could once more ply my trade was recompense enough. However, when first-class passengers got wind of "the ship's hairdresser," as I was soon referred to, and requested my services, I changed my policy. By the end of the voyage, I had earned enough money to have crossed the Atlantic twice—in cabin class!

By the time the *Gustav Nachtigal* reached Boston after eleven weeks, I had learned a great deal about Erika's life. Having regained the power of speech, she made full use of it thereafter. Life in her uncle's family, which had prospered from the importation of cotton, was dominated by a single subject: America. For anyone with business sense and enough drive and initiative, her uncle declared, the sky was the limit there. Although one still had to cope with pigheaded natives, and, as her uncle said, the work ethic of the Africans specially imported to pick cotton required improvement, business was already booming.

He took Erika to visit his warehouses, in which bales of cotton were stacked ready for forwarding to countries all over Europe, and allowed her to feel the soft white bolls with her fingers. What fascinated her even more than their beauty was the thought that they had last been touched by a black hand. She felt she could almost touch that hand and feel its skin.

When Erika was twelve, her uncle apprenticed her to a hairdressing salon. It was patronized almost exclusively by men who came to have their beards and mustaches trimmed, and it was Erika's job to sweep up the trimmings. She learned a lot about life, politics, and business, because the customers had barely sat down before they let fly. Women very seldom visited the salon, which was why she had been able to read my thoughts the first time we met. Whenever they did, her master had looked as entranced as I had when eying her hair across the table.

Although she was never given anything more responsible to do than sweep up hair, Erika had grasped over the years that hairdressers differed from all other manual workers in that their task consisted of helping people to harmonize their outward appearance with their inner self. For many, this was clearly a magical moment, because when her employer had done an especially good job, they examined themselves in the mirror for several seconds, reduced to silence, then left the salon as if they had just been reborn.

Erika blushed when I told her I had never heard a more wonderful description of my craft. From that day on, she was always present whenever I cut a passenger's hair, and she swept up the trimmings.

Our ways parted in Boston. Erika booked a seat on a train bound for New York, whereas I decided to stay put. On my first reconnaissance of the city, my eye was caught by a notice in a barbershop window. It was advertising—in German—for a hairdresser.

The owner of the salon was a man from Detmold named Eugen Dröscher. He received me lying on a chaise longue in the back room, whither I was conducted by his humpbacked little wife. Her husband was sick, very sick, she said as she drew back the curtain that divided the premises in two. Dröscher was around sixty years old and must once have been a fine figure of a man. His feet projected beyond the end of the couch, and his massive head reposed on a rolled-up woolen blanket. His face was gaunt, and the eyes that looked up at me were watery. He suffered from gout in his hands, his wife told me. His fingers were so painful sometimes, he was unable to sleep for days on end and couldn't even raise the energy to eat. Holding scissors and comb was out of the question. He'd been like this for weeks, and their customers had gone elsewhere, not that you could blame them. Unless someone could be found who would run the salon until her husband recovered his strength, they would have to close. Eugen Dröscher gazed at me sadly and said nothing.

I turned up for work the next morning. Unfortunately, though, no customers appeared. I stood outside the door for a week, watching the comings and goings on the street and resolving to learn English as quickly as possible. An opportunity to do so soon arose in the shape of a young woman from the neighborhood who did the Dröschers' shopping for them. Of German descent herself, she was called Judith Waiszmann. Her family had lived in America for two generations, and her knowledge of German was just sufficient to enable her to understand the bare essentials. She had been caught in a sudden downpour before she entered the salon, and although her hair was bedraggled, I saw at once how soft and supple it was. She was about to leave when I advised her not to brave the rain again and have her hair done by me instead.

She said she had no money, and besides, she always cut her own hair. Eugen Dröscher called out from behind the curtain that his salon was a men's-only establishment, but his words were drowned out by a violent clap of thunder that made the barbershop window and Judith Waiszmann tremble in equal measure.

"You see," I told her, "someone up there doesn't want you to go." I led her over to the chair and she sat down, still trembling. Then I made a proposal I'd been turning over in my mind for several minutes: she wouldn't pay, I would. She should regard herself as my model, and if she didn't like my work, I would pay her twice the original fee as compensation.

Judith did not reply, but she let me have my way. She watched in the mirror as I molded her hair into one of the boldest creations I had ever designed: the projecting cones over her ears converged at the back of her head into a point that was vaguely reminiscent of a ship's bow. Above the cones, I tapered the hair into a sort of canopy over her face that terminated in a highland plateau on which reposed yet another cone. I was so engrossed in my work, I did not at first notice that Eugen Dröscher had risen from his couch and was standing beside me.

When I had finished, he raised his gouty hand, pointed to the wall, and said, "Look!" The rain had stopped, and a sunbeam was bathing Judith's coiffure in a golden glow. The shadow it projected on the wall resembled an enormous painting.

The following day, she returned with two young women whom she introduced as her friends, and who wanted the same hairstyle. The day after that, more women—friends of Judith Waiszmann's friends—appeared. On the third day, Amalie Dröscher had to draw up a list on which yet more women—friends of friends of Judith Waiszmann's friends—entered their names. Although I worked without a break until late at night, the last of them had to wait a week and did so without demur. Many of them turned up long before their appointments just to watch their friends having their hair done, with the result that the salon was thronged with young women all day long, and a crowd gathered outside the window. Street traders took advantage of this to sell soft drinks and cookies. Neighbors brought chairs for the elderly to sit on, and the horse-drawn trolley added an extra stop to its route to enable passengers to survey the scene.

Then the salon received a visit from two men who introduced themselves as reporters from the *Boston Globe*. While one of them interviewed me and busily made notes, the other sketched me and Judith Waiszmann, who had come to do the shopping for Amalie Dröscher.

I was impressed by his skill. He captured Judith's hairstyle perfectly and produced an excellent likeness of me. When the report appeared in the paper, I became a celebrity overnight, albeit a controversial one. I was surprised to read that the reporter had also interviewed people on the street outside, and that they had made critical and even hostile comments to the effect that the Germans had disturbed the peace, not for the first time, by inciting women to immoral behavior. Certain city councilors, when shown the drawing of Judith's hairstyle, reacted with outrage and demanded that its propriety be made the subject of a debate in council. It should be added, in the reporter's favor, that some approving and enthusiastic comments were also printed. The following day, the *Boston Globe* printed a whole page on which local citizens expressed their opinions, positive and negative in equal numbers.

Far from pouring oil on troubled waters, however, this merely added fuel to the flames, and weekend demonstrations were announced by both camps. In the preceding days, citizens armed with placards stationed themselves outside the salon. On the morning of the demonstrations, I received a visit from a plainclothes policeman who suggested that I spend the next forty-eight hours in police custody for my own protection. Judith Waiszmann and several of her friends had already been taken into protective custody, he told me, and he advised the Dröschers to close the salon and lower the metal shutters.

I must unreservedly commend the Boston police for their hospitality. While the demonstrators were marching through the streets and converging on the salon, where they chanted their slogans but refrained from coming to blows, we were being entertained with coffee and cake at police headquarters. We were also allowed some lady visitors, these being the wives of senior police officers and politicians desirous of seeing the corpus delicti at close quarters and of making my acquaintance. By the end of the two days, I had received requests from ten society women to restyle their hair.

Public agitation subsided as quickly as it had arisen. Americans were like that, the police commissioner explained when saying goodbye to me: volatile, but solidarity always triumphed in the end. In the Old World, a dispute of this kind would doubtless have led to war, so I was absolutely right to seek my future in this glorious land. Any young man with new ideas was welcome, he said, even if they weren't to everyone's taste.

When I went back to work on Monday morning, the barbershop was full of elderly gentlemen in need of a shave. The customers had returned, and Eugen Dröscher, whose gout had miraculously cured itself, was hard put to answer all their questions about recent events. His salon was now an attraction featured by tourist brochures for foreign visitors.

I had acquired a certain notoriety too. The *Boston Herald* offered me a column in its weekend edition in which I was to discuss questions of etiquette and aesthetics and present new hairstyles, to be depicted in his usual style by the artist of my acquaintance, who had since gone over to the *Globe*'s competitor. I was told that the American public needed unconventional ideas and suggestions to prevent them from becoming as outdated as the Old World. The *Herald* had taken up this cause, and I was the ideal figurehead.

My first column dealt with the question of inward and outward identity and potential ways of expressing one's personality through attributes such as hairstyles, and, of course, I cited the German philosopher Erika America, who had immigrated to New York. Accompanying my article was an illustration of the coiffure I had designed for her on board the *Gustav Nachtigal.* This column attracted great attention and a widespread response. The Boston Women's Association invited me to participate in an evening discussion group and tell them more about Erika and other Old World intellectuals; a group of Boston artists offered to display my creations in their studio; and soon afterward my tussocks were accorded their first public exhibition, side by side with paintings and sculptures.

Another of my columns examined the question of how hairstyles could promote communication and social assimilation. And in yet another, I advanced the theory that the way in which human beings wear their hair had made a substantial contribution to cultural development. None of the hairstyles illustrated evoked a reaction comparable to Judith Waiszmann's in the *Globe*, probably because the *Herald*'s circulation was far smaller. The paper folded after my fifth column, but I was assured that this was not my fault; but for me, it would probably have done so sooner.

This loss did not hit me particularly hard. I had used my fees to rent a modest studio in which I lived and worked on my tussocks. It became a rendezvous point for Boston society ladies who wanted coiffures that would attract attention to themselves on festive occasions.

I soon felt thoroughly at home in Boston. The city was well laid out—the streets were wide, the buildings new, and the people considerate. Whenever I paused at an intersection, wondering which way to go, someone would offer to help. When their offer foundered on my inadequate knowledge of the language, they didn't take it amiss but gave me a friendly pat on the back and wished me luck. Fortunately, I often received visits from Judith, who familiarized me with the English language and offered to continue to act as my model. This facilitated my work with clients because I could demonstrate my ideas to them with the aid of Judith's extremely versatile hair. They had no objection to paying her for this service, so she gave up her activities as a shopper and maid-of-all-work and spent most of the day with me. After three months, she moved in full-time.

One day, Erika appeared at my door. She had thoroughly disliked her time at the home of her uncle's business acquaintance, she told me. Everything there revolved around the sale and resale of cotton pickers. She had often been obliged to accompany him to the harbor when human cargo arrived and needed inspecting. Ragged, half-starved figures had crawled out of the hatches over the holds, and a dentist had peered into their mouths before they were shipped on elsewhere. Now and again, her employer would pick out a particularly sturdy African and put him to work in his home, making the poor creature sleep in a dog kennel behind the house. On top of everything else, she had developed an allergy to raw cotton and had grown tired of her hairstyle. That was why she had come.

So the three of us set up home together in my studio, and it proved very practical for me to have another model at my disposal. Better still, I taught both young women to wield comb and scissors, so we were soon able to practice a division of labor: I would design the creations and, provided they were not too complicated, the other two would put them into effect.

We were more and more often requested to call on customers and do their hair in the evenings, either immediately before a party or for no particular reason. On such occasions, a group of women friends would get together and the hairdressing itself became a regular event, with food and drink and jollification that often went on into the wee hours. Mrs. Penelope Parker was the first to hit on the idea of sending out written invitations to a gathering of this kind, calling it a "Skrik Party." It was such a success that Skrik Parties were soon being held all over Boston, and I had trouble keeping up with the demand for my services.

A woman friend of Judith's took on the job of coordinating my bookings because I was so fully occupied at the studio during the day. Business there was extremely brisk too—so brisk that I trained more friends of Judith's to use brushes and combs and opened several branches. After a year, there were seven Skriks in Boston. I couldn't be in all those salons at once, of course, so I continued to concentrate on the studio, where I personally attended to select regular customers, and I visited one branch a day to pass on suggestions and advice.

One snowy winter morning, Amalie Dröscher came to the studio. It seemed her husband was suffering from renewed spells of gout and couldn't attend to his customers, so she asked if I could help out again. The upshot was that I spent the weeks before Christmas trimming beards in Eugen Dröscher's barbershop. He was in a really bad way. It wasn't just his hands this time—his whole body hurt, and he was visibly in pain as he lay on his couch behind the curtain. I did whatever I could, taking over the shopping now that Judith wasn't available and helping Amalie Dröscher to wash her husband and change his clothes. I enjoyed those days in his barbershop, with its tranquil routine and the little conversations I had with customers from the neighborhood who came for a shave every morning. Eugen Dröscher died on Christmas Eve. From his couch, he had just seen the last customer leave and watched me sweep up beard trimmings while the gas lamps were being lit outside and children trooped past singing carols. Then he closed his eyes.

After the funeral, I escorted his widow home. Before saying goodbye, we stood together in the semidarkness of the silent barbershop, whose yellowed walls seemed to whisper all the stories that had been told within them. I said I envied Eugen the life he had been privileged to lead there, but Amalie Dröscher told me she didn't intend to remain in the place a day longer than necessary. There was nothing to keep her there anymore, she said, and she wanted to spend the evening of her days back home in Detmold, where her sister's family lived. All she doubted was whether she could manage to undertake the long voyage on her own.

I told her that I wouldn't mind keeping her company and would book us passage on one of the new, fast sailing ships, which I did the following day. It was the *Liberty*.

# 22

## *You can only close the door if you stay*

At noon on the forty-sixth day of the voyage, a seagull hovered above the *Liberty*'s masthead. This herald and scout from the nearby continent made an elegant landing on the sundeck, waddled to and fro a few times, hopped onto a deck chair, and peered through the window into the dining saloon, where lunch was just being served.

Maria Tommasi di Bibione, who was the first to notice it, sprang to her feet and let out a high A. "A-A-A-America!" she cried, pointing to the bird, which cocked its head and gave her a one-eyed stare. In a trice, everyone jumped up and dashed outside.

But America wasn't yet in evidence. Stretching ahead of the ship from bow to horizon was the usual gray expanse of water. Necks were craned, binoculars raised, excited cries uttered. This commotion brought the second-class passengers up on deck, and within minutes the fo'c'sle was crowded with people. The seagull rose into the air with provocative deliberation, hovered above their heads for a moment, released a big white blob of excrement, and flew off in the direction it had come from. It had seen enough: another shipload of people on their way in hopes of lending their lives new meaning.

Odysseus Hirsch and I stood in the wheelhouse and watched the seagull depart. It would be evening at the earliest before the longed-for green ribbon appeared on the horizon, and even then it would be hours before we reached land—hours that often seemed longer than the whole of the time that had gone before. Impatience could easily turn to ill humor; the crew knew that. On one previous voyage, the tension had become so great that a passenger took the helmsman hostage in the belief that he had secretly turned back and demanded to get to America in an hour at most. On such occasions, one had to rely on the captain's experience. He told the passenger he was absolutely right, thanked him for having finally exposed the perfidious helmsman's underhanded conduct, and asked for his help in locking the offender up in a storeroom. When the captain returned, the hostage taker was in irons and the helmsman lighting his pipe in the wheelhouse.

In order to avoid such explosive situations, the captain, whose name was Baldur Bellmann, had devised an entertainment program he christened "Magic Hours"—an allusion to the few remaining hours of the voyage. As on previous occasions, he now invited everyone to come and watch his conjuring tricks in the saloon—including the second-class passengers. They would see things they would remember all their lives, he said, and he promised them that land would come in sight before his magic show was over: he would conjure America into being.

The saloon was soon full to bursting. After a few harmless conjuring tricks that delighted the children, the captain progressed to more demanding feats of deception, culminating in the main attraction: the disappearing trick. Did anyone have the courage to volunteer for it? he asked. The guinea pig had always reappeared in the past, but one never knew . . .

Nobody spoke up, and since I was standing in his immediate vicinity, his eye fell on me. I wasn't standing there by chance, of course. Nobody had ever volunteered, so the role of guinea pig regularly devolved upon a member of the crew. Usually me.

When the spectators saw that I was in the firing line, I pretended to be scared. This prompted them to spur me on, and the saloon soon rang with cries of "Skrik! Skrik! Skrik!" That left me no choice.

So I let Baldur Bellmann shut me up in a cabinet constructed especially for this trick. After securing the door with several padlocks, he asked the audience to satisfy themselves that there was no second exit, so I couldn't get out. Meanwhile, I quietly slid aside a thin partition and squeezed into the rear compartment of the cabinet, then closed it so the interior would appear empty when the door was opened.

The audience conducted a thorough examination that convinced them all was in order. Then, after uttering some magic spells, Baldur Bellmann opened the door. My disappearance was greeted with loud applause. Now came the harder part, he said: magicking me back. He locked the door again and muttered more spells. Meantime, I tried to slide the partition open, but it jammed. When the door opened again, I was nowhere to be seen.

I was still in the rear compartment of the cabinet after three incantations. Silent at first, the audience grew restless, and even Baldur Bellmann found it hard to conceal his bewilderment. I heard him walk around the cabinet several times. That was enough, he hissed—the next time he opened the cabinet, I'd better be there. Just then, earsplitting cries of jubilation rent the air: "America!" Land had evidently been sighted on the horizon, and everyone trooped out onto the foredeck.

The captain opened the cabinet again, and I still wasn't there. He was going to break the back off, he told me indignantly. At the same moment, my efforts were rewarded at last and I was able to squeeze into the main compartment, sliding the partition shut behind me. When Bellmann levered off the back of the cabinet with the help of several seamen, I wasn't there either. "Skrik!" he cried. "My God, what have I done!"

Serge told me later that the captain had thereupon clutched his chest and slumped to the floor.

Now that it didn't matter anymore, I summarily smashed the partition and climbed out through the shattered back of the cabinet. I found the captain lying at my feet and Dr. Heimo Servatius kneeling beside him, massaging his thorax. His exertions bore fruit a few minutes later, when Baldur Bellmann emitted a deep sigh and opened his eyes.

New York welcomed us in the best of spirits. Brilliant sunshine made the surface of the harbor basin sparkle, the quayside looked immaculate, the waiting crowd waved little flags, and the strident strains of a brass band came drifting across the water. The *Liberty* herself was not to be outdone. Under the direction of the Wild West author, passengers on the foredeck were performing a surprise dance that he had entitled "Hope and Goodwill Entering the New World." Pernille Jakobsson, attired in a white leotard, was juggling with the *Liberty*'s anchors to the singing of Maria Tommasi di Bibione, who was performing an aria from Lehár's *The Land of Smiles* accompanied by Vladimir Gospodin and the nuns' choir, while Oleg Krassimov shadowboxed in time to the music. Dr. Heinrich Birnbaum had put top hats on his three remaining macaques, which were turning cartwheels on the back of the ewe that owed her survival to the vines; and the lacemakers were clattering their wooden needles together. In the midst of all this activity stood the Wild West author, dressed as a trapper and rhythmically raising and lowering a fake scalp.

Odysseus Hirsch and I were standing in the wheelhouse watching this performance as the *Liberty* slowly glided toward the jubilant crowd on the quay. At that moment, a hoarse blare from astern made us spin around. I was still turning to discover its source when a vast shadow engulfed the *Liberty*.

"The *Gigantic*," said Odysseus. "She's back! So that's why all those people are waiting down there."

"And she's going much too fast again," I cried out as the huge ship's black hull loomed up beside us. Odysseus spun his wheel wildly to increase the distance between the two vessels, but, as the *Gigantic* glided past, her bow wave came surging over the *Liberty*'s side and, with an almighty splash, rained down on her deck.

Passengers usually couldn't wait to go ashore, but disembarkation was delayed this time. More than a dozen bedraggled ladies crowded into my salon for me to repair at least some of the ravages inflicted on their hair. Countess Urbach, who was warmly applauded, declared that they owed it to the Old World's reputation, whatever else one might think of it. "Do your best, Skrik—Europe's prestige is in your hands."

Later, Odysseus and I stood at the rail and watched the passengers line up outside the immigration building, many of them swaying and unsteady on their feet. "Want a look?" he asked, handing me his telescope.

There was a lot of jostling when the passengers from the *Gigantic* also came ashore. Those waiting in line cast envious glances at the fortunate souls who brandished their immigration papers as they emerged from the other door of the building. No one had been refused entry, it seemed. I saw the nuns and the lacemakers performing a sort of Indian dance; the zoologist kissed each of his monkeys in turn, and Pernille Jakobsson was welcomed by representatives of the Ringling Bros. Circus, who had brought a camel on which she rode, waving to the crowd, while the pianist panted along beside her carrying her dumbbells. Countess Urbach had found some porters to convey her mysterious trunk to a waiting carriage. Betty von Reventlow and Adolphe Durand left the quayside arm in arm, the Dagorne brothers had persuaded the Wild West author and Oleg Krassimov to help them carry their vines, and Ernest and Helen Basil and their four children hurried past them in single file. Guillermo Scalatti reverently held the door open for La Tommasi, who was soon followed by the Hütterlis. No one else emerged for a while.

"I guess you'll be packing up your things today," said Odysseus Hirsch.

I shook my head. A brand-new, fully equipped salon was waiting for me on board the *Gigantic*, I explained. Whoever succeeded me on the *Liberty* need not worry about equipment, as mine would all remain on board—as a bequest, so to speak.

Odysseus pointed to the immigration building. "There's someone else coming out," he said.

I raised the telescope and saw Franziska von Hausendorf emerge into the open. "Raimund will never recognize her like that," I said. "I'll explain later," I added when Odysseus looked puzzled. Then I went ashore.

Franziska gave a start when I came up beside her. There were no spies or agents around, I assured her. She could take off her disguise, or Raimund would have no hope of recognizing her—if he was there. She bore little resemblance to herself even when she removed her man's cap. That was no problem, she replied; *she* would recognize *him*, and she sensed he was somewhere nearby. I offered to help her look for somewhere to stay for the night, and we soon found her a boardinghouse.

On the way back, I strolled through the twilit side streets of New York. Because I knew them well from my many previous visits with the *Liberty*, I was surprised to spot a little barbershop I'd never noticed before. The light was still on inside, so I crossed the street and looked in. A woman was reading a newspaper in one of the two barber's chairs. To judge by her smock, she was the proprietress. She wore pebble-lensed glasses and was holding the paper close to her eyes. Then I caught sight of a sign on the door. It bore the name *Erica America* in faded lettering.

Going inside, I stood there irresolutely for a moment or two. There were some yellowing newspaper clippings from the *Boston Herald* pinned to the walls, I noticed. Without looking up from her paper, Erika said, "You can only close the door if you stay this time."

I softly closed the door.

I have now been living in New York for five years. The *Liberty* has been broken up for scrap, and the *Gigantic* disappeared during a hurricane in the Bermuda Triangle. Franziska von Hausendorf, who has regrown her magnificent head of hair, is still waiting for Raimund and still senses that he is quite nearby. Erika and I invite her to lunch on Sundays. She always sits on the straw-filled pillow she carries everywhere, ready to give it to Raimund as soon as he appears.

# *About the Author*

*Photo © 2010 Paul Schirnhofer, Agentur Focus*

Karsten Flohr was born in 1950 in Hamburg, where he lives today. After training with and then editing the daily newspaper *Hamburger Abendblatt*, he worked for various periodicals, including *Petra* and *Brigitte*, and as editor in chief of *Vital*, *TV Today*, and *Woman*. Since 2005, Flohr has been working as a science journalist.

# *About the Translator*

*Photo © Sherbourne Photographic*

Originally a classicist whose school diet from age eight included ancient Greek as well as Latin, John Brownjohn won a major scholarship to Oxford, whence he graduated with honors. Thereafter, partly because he hails from a ramified family whose members fought on both sides during World War II, he made the transition to modern languages and a career as a literary translator, which has earned him critical acclaim and many British and American awards. In addition to translating the better part of two hundred books, he has produced English versions of many German and French screenplays and cowritten several feature films with Roman Polanski.

Made in the USA
Monee, IL
22 June 2026

55338454R00105